Bay in the Dark

Bay in the Dark

Sharon Henegar

Saturday Books

Published by Saturday Books
3160 Holiday Dr. S.
Salem, OR 97302

ISBN 978-0-9961980-3-5
Henegar, Sharon L.
Bay in the Dark / Sharon L. Henegar
McGuire, Louisa (Fictitious Character)—Fiction
Dogs—Fiction
Humorous Fiction
Mystery Fiction

Book 4: Willow Falls series

Dedicated to
Diana Roberts,
and our friendship that
defies mathematics.
How can we have known each other
for over forty years when we ourselves
are somewhere around thirty-five?

Bay in the Dark

1

The tiny pocket park was a welcome sight. I headed straight for the shade-dappled bench that was perfectly situated under the spreading branches of a venerable oak and sank down gratefully on the slatted seat. My greyhound, Emily Ann, subsided into an alert down pose at my feet with an audible sigh. Jack, our low-slung long-eared friend (he of the mixed Labrador and Basset parentage) remained standing, the better to wag at passersby.

I had forgotten how warm the Bay Area could be in September. I'd been lured into a longer walk than I had intended by the dogs' enthusiasm and my enjoyment of the houses and front yards in this Berkeley neighborhood.

The lovely, oh-so-hilly neighborhood.

Next to walking through a forest, hills might be my least favorite terrain to traverse on foot.

"At least there aren't any barbed wire fences to climb over. Or under." I spoke aloud, and both dogs looked at me, heads cocked. "Or vines that attack you. Or underbrush. Okay, I feel better already."

I also felt a long way from home, which indeed I was. The dogs and I had spent five days in my old Civic hatchback crossing the vast expanses between my house in the Midwest and my boyfriend Bob's little cottage in the Berkeley hills. The trip seemed like a journey through another time, passing through the prairies and mountain forests and deserts of the West. The rugged landscape spoke to me of patience and endurance. It was the same today as it had been when I was born, or eons ago.

I was in no hurry. In fact, there were reasons I wished we might never arrive at our destination. Each day I devised a route that might include places for the dogs to run, not caring if we went out of our way. We had visited dog parks in four states, and a few times I found deserted places off side roads to get in a good run. (The dogs, not me. I watched.)

A couple of rabbits in southern Wyoming are probably still recounting to their cousins the story of how cleverly they escaped the two monsters that chased them. I imagined them years from now, old and gray and boring the baby rabbits to tears with their well-worn tale, in which Jack and Emily Ann had grown to the size of elephants. Fast elephants.

I still felt bad about those bunnies. But at least there had been no tragic ending—and the dogs had been ecstatic at their adventure.

"I don't think you'll find much wildlife to menace here in the wilds of Berkeley," I told my companions.

"At least, not of the four-footed variety. But Bob said he'd take us to a dog park tomorrow. For today you will have to make do with me."

Jack sat down and panted lovingly at me. I smiled back, and blinked away the tears that sprang to my eyes.

One day on our trip west, I had emerged from some daydream and realized I was heading due north. Toward Canada. Away from California. Because Jack was Bob's dog, and I had promised to return him. Because Bob wanted me, as well as Jack, to make my home there. And because I knew I loved Bob, but not if I loved him enough. But it was time to find out, and so we had turned south.

A Sousa march began to play from my jacket pocket, and I fished out my phone. No need to check to see who was calling.

"Hi, Kay."

"Hey, Louisa! Are you there? What's it like? How's Bob? Any protests going on? Do you like it? Are you—"

"Kay, slow down! First of all, weren't the protests you're thinking of about forty years ago? And yes, we got here late yesterday. Sorry I didn't call you. We had to do all the greeting stuff, and we went out to dinner soon after we arrived, and when I did start to call I remembered the time difference and it was awfully late."

"The greeting stuff, huh." She gave a dirty snicker.

"Stop. Not going there."

"Dang. You are just so private."

3

"And don't you forget it. Besides, your imagination is far more lurid than anything Bob or I would ever, um, come up with. I don't want to ruin your fantasies."

"I bet that's not true. Someday you're going to break down and tell me everything and then we'll find out who has the lurid imagination."

"You just go right on thinking that, cuz."

"Anyway, tell me everything. Is it a nice day? My weather app says you've got sunshine."

"Sunshine and close to ninety degrees. Why did I think September would mean fall weather?"

"I guess you've forgotten what it's like there."

"Kay, I left here before I was a year old. You weren't even born yet when my parents took me to Willow Falls. So no, I do not remember the weather patterns."

"Excuses, excuses. Anyway, what are you doing right now? Is Bob there? Can I tell him hello?"

"He's working. He—"

"Working? How can he be working? You just got there."

"Yes, well, he had two clients already booked, and he's recording an interview later that was set up ages ago. Oddly enough, the world does not stop when I get to town."

"Baloney. Bob's world should stop when you get to town. You haven't seen him for months."

"Bob at least recognizes that I need a certain amount of time to myself, even if some cousins who shall remain nameless do not."

"I am well aware of your tendencies to be a hermit, believe me. So if Bob's at work, where are you?"

"Took the dogs for a walk. And walked and walked. You would absolutely love this neighborhood. Great old houses in all kinds of styles, and the landscaping is amazing. Apparently practically anything will grow here."

"Louisa, you know nothing about plants."

"True, but that doesn't mean I can't appreciate them. And I do know a rose when I see it. And daisies. And irises. And—"

"Stop! I take it all back. You are a walking encyclopedia of horticultural knowledge."

"I've got to find out what these tall trees with blue leaves are though. They smell like cough drops."

"They have trees that smell like cough drops? Maybe they're cherry trees."

"No, silly, not pieces of candy pretending to be cough drops. The kind of cough drops that blast your nasal passages open. Oh, I know, I bet these are eucalyptus trees."

"Eucalyptus? I thought those grew in Australia. Did you take a wrong turn somewhere? Only you could head out for California and end up in Australia. Do you see any kangaroos? Or koalas?"

"Nope, all I see is a young woman pushing a tandem stroller with a baby and a two year old in it. And cars going by. And—"

"And houses and cement and sky. Got it."

"I'm sitting on a bench in the world's smallest park, taking a breather. They have hills here."

Kay knows how I feel about hills. "Poor baby." She almost managed to sound genuinely sympathetic. "How far are you from Bob's place?"

"I'm not really sure. We've been winding around. Could be a block, could be a mile. In a minute I'm going to return to my feet and walk down to the busy street I can see from here and find a place to have lunch. Bob said lots of places have patios and sidewalk tables that allow dogs."

"Well, I still think he was remiss not to cancel everything at least for your first day there, but you do sound like you're having a good time."

"I am, really. And you know what they say..." She joined in to chant the rest of the sentence with me, and I knew we were both rolling our eyes in an identical manner. "...it's all good."

We giggled at each other, and said goodbye. As I stowed the phone back in my pocket I said to the dogs, "That was your Auntie Kay, as you probably could hear. She misses you." I gathered up their leashes and leaned forward so I could stand. As I got to my feet, Jack jumped up and barked once, and I realized both dogs were on the alert and watching something down the hill from us. I followed their gaze and saw a fluffy-tailed squirrel scampering up the sidewalk toward us. Close behind the squirrel was a small floofy black dog, intent on its prey, leash flying. Halfway down the block, a tall woman made even taller by high heels was running up the hill, yelling.

6

"Daphne! Daphne! Come! Dammit, get your hairy little ass back here!"

Behind me, the sound of an accelerating vehicle grew closer. The panicked squirrel suddenly realized it was running full tilt toward two more dogs. It made an instantaneous ninety degree turn into the street. Brakes screeched.

Small floofy dog was not expecting the turn and overshot. It put on its brakes so it could turn to follow the squirrel. Adrenaline shot through me. I shouted, "Stop!" and lunged forward. Somehow my foot came down on the leash and stayed there long enough for the dog to be rudely jerked back when it hit the end of its tether, just before it reached the street. I teetered and almost fell, but managed to grab the leash and right myself. The squirrel finished his mad dash with a willowy leap that took him halfway up the trunk of a gigantic oak tree, where he disappeared among the leaves.

The driver of the car, a middle aged woman with spiky hair, glared through her open window. "If you can't keep control of your dogs, you shouldn't have so many," she yelled at us before starting down the hill again, though at a slower pace than before.

I gaped after her. Did she think that was another dog that ran across the street and jumped into a tree? Jeez, and I thought I didn't know anything about wildlife.

The dog's owner panted her way up to us. "Oh. My. God." She fell onto the bench I had just vacated. Her unrepentant pet jumped into her lap, wagging its plume of a tail and kissing her chin. "Oh, god. Thank you." She made an effort to catch her breath, and reached out for her dog's leash. I handed it over.

"Are you okay? I'd be having a heart attack if it had been one of my dogs about to get run over."

She waved her free hand in front of her face and took a deep breath. "I have only myself to blame. I was trying to send a text to a client and I wasn't paying attention. Oh, Daphne, you silly girl." She leaned over to plant a return kiss on the small head, and I used the moment to survey them both.

The woman, who I guessed to be in her mid-forties, had curly shoulder-length dark hair and brown eyes. She was dressed entirely in leopard print clothing—shirt, jeans, sleeveless jacket, high heeled boots, even a beret. I blinked, wondering where one could find that much leopard apparel. Not, I was sure, in Willow Falls.

Daphne was indubitably a dog, but she was either some rare breed I'd never encountered or a mix that produced huge upstanding ears made even larger by waving wisps of long black hair. She was covered with the same soft fur, and her curved tail was as extravagantly plumed as her ears.

Daphne's owner took another deep breath. "All right, I think I'm going to skip the heart attack this time. Daphne, you are a wicked, wicked child to scare me like that. You must promise me you will never chase another squirrel."

If Daphne promised, I was sure she had her fingers crossed. Her pink tongue fell out of her mouth in a happy, completely unrepentant pant. She turned around on her owner's lap to look at my dogs, then hopped down to exchange greetings. Her owner and I wore goofy grins watching them. All three handled the customary nose touches in fine style. The ritual butt sniffs took longer due to the extreme difference in their sizes.

Finally the woman gripped the leash more tightly and stood. "I don't suppose there's any chance you'd let me buy you lunch or a drink or something by way of thanks?"

I smiled up at her. "I was just going to look for somewhere to eat."

"Brilliant. I know just the place, and it's right around the corner."

2

I settled into the comfortable chair and looked around, feeling strangely at home. In a moment I realized that this restaurant patio was arranged very much like the one at the Bluebird Cafe back in Willow Falls. I hoped the food would be as good.

Emily Ann and Jack were old hands at how to behave on restaurant patios. They settled on either side of my chair, relaxed but watchful for any falling tidbits. Daphne sniffed the table legs, and then the chair legs. Her owner caught her attention and raised an eyebrow. The dog immediately circled twice and curled into a small package. The ears remained upstanding and alert. I smiled and shook my head.

"Those ears! I've never seen anything like her."

"I know. I've always wondered if I could use her in place of a satellite dish."

"Is she a mix or some breed I don't know?"

"Oh, honey, she's a mutt," laughed the woman. "I'm guessing there's some Yorkie in her background, and maybe Maltese, and those ears look like a Papillon's, but she could be anything. I'm too cheap to do that DNA test they've got now. I mean, who cares?"

"Jack is like that," I said, looking down at him. He was watching me and thumped his strong, thick tail. "We think he's a Basset-Labrador mix, but you never really know. I'm Louisa McGuire, by the way."

"Penny Marquette." She held out her hand over the table and we shook. Her grip was warm, with just the right pressure. "So. Do you live here in the neighborhood, Louisa?"

"No, I'm visiting a friend for a few days. I live in Willow Falls, Missouri."

"Wow, long way from home."

Our server arrived. Her short bob was striped with purple and pink dyes, and she sported enough piercings and tattoos to declare her lack of fear about pain. She gave us a shiny-toothed smile as she handed over menus.

"Hi, Penny, nice to see you and Daphne."

"Thanks, Ashley. This is my new friend Louisa."

Ashley turned the full wattage of her smile on me. "Hi, Louisa. Welcome. I see you came with an entourage."

"Thanks. Yes, this is Emily Ann, and this is Jack."

"I'll see what I can find in the way of dog biscuits. I know the baker was making some earlier."

"What's good today?" Penny asked. "Besides the dog biscuits, of course."

"I had a bowl of the potato leek soup earlier, and it is to *die* for. Vegetarian, but not vegan. The vegan special is the chilaquiles, which are simmered in a spicy tomato salsa and then drizzled with cashew crema, cilantro and avocado, with black beans on the side. Julie's also made up some nettle and sheep's milk ricotta ravioli. Oh, and you might want to save room for the passionfruit meringues. Would you like a few minutes to look at the menu?"

I wanted to fall back in my chair and moan with delight. Penny said, "Gosh, everything sounds good. Yeah, give us a minute."

Ashley nodded and hurried away. I opened my menu and started to read.

"Lord have mercy." I shook my head. Penny looked at me enquiringly. "Everything sounds wonderful. Maybe I could just eat a few of the descriptions."

She chuckled. "I know. And unlike a lot of menu prose, the food actually lives up to the hype."

We both studied the menus. In a few minutes Ashley returned and we ordered—that soup for me, and a salad for Penny that included roasted Brussels sprouts and sweet peppers, pumpkin, pomegranate and pine nuts. I realized I was starving, and that the scrambled egg and English muffin I had eaten with Bob that morning had been several hours ago. "I'm ravenous," I admitted.

"It won't take long to get fed," Penny assured me. "I live nearby and come here often, and I think they must all wear roller skates in the kitchen, they work so fast. Now where were we? Oh yes, Willow Falls. Where is it? The name sounds familiar somehow."

I tried not to cringe, hoping she didn't remember any of the stupid things that had been on the news. "It's roughly halfway between Kansas City and St. Louis. Very small. I grew up there, then lived in Seattle for a long time, then moved back after my husband died."

There. The truth. But not the whole truth.

"And what do you do in Willow Falls?"

"I help my cousin in her antique store, and hang out with my dogs. You?"

"I'm an arson investigator."

I'm afraid I goggled at her. "Really?"

"Yes, really."

"Sorry. I've just always had this fantasy of telling a chance-met stranger some complete lie about what I do, like casually whipping out that I'm the embroidery correspondent for the Kansas City *Star*."

"I like that. I may borrow it sometime."

"Please do. Arson. Wow. So is Daphne your arson detection dog?"

Now it was her turn to goggle. "Well, yes. She is. But no one has ever said that before. Even if they have heard of arson dogs, they assume they're all honkin' big Labs."

I lifted the edge of the starched white tablecloth to peek at Daphne. She was still curled into a ball, but the huge ears swiveled as she took in the sounds around us. "I would think a dog her size would be really useful. She could get into places a Lab couldn't."

"Exactly!"

"And I bet her nose is just as good." I looked at the small nose in question. "You got a good nose, Miss Daphne?"

The dog raised her head from her paws to look at me and gave a quiet, "Woof."

"That sounds like a yes to me." I dropped the tablecloth and sat back, just as Ashley returned with a large tray balanced on one hand and a folded rack in the other. She deftly flipped open the rack and deposited the tray on it. "Wow. That was fast."

"I figure folks who get here at the end of lunch time are probably extra hungry," Ashley chuckled, and deposited an enormous bowl of steaming, silky soup of the palest green in front of me. She slid Penny's plate onto the table, then a basket with several types of bread between us. A generous pot of soft butter went next to the bread. She refilled our water glasses. Finally, a small plate that with an assortment of crunchy-looking tidbits was placed in front of each dog. Jack and Emily Ann looked up at me, and when I nodded they inhaled their treats.

"All righty then. Anything else you need just now?"

She sounded exactly like Cleta, our favorite waitress at the Bluebird Cafe. We assured her everything was wonderful, and almost as whole heartedly as the dogs we fell upon our food. The soup was everything Ashley had said.

"My gosh, Penny, this is wonderful."

"I know, I know. I have zero incentive to cook for myself since I found this place."

14

"We have the Bluebird Cafe at home which believe it or not is just as good. My cousin Kay and I eat there nearly every day."

"This is your cousin with the antique store?"

"That's the one. My only cousin, actually my only relative."

"Whereas I have relatives up the wazoo. Would you like some? I have several I would gladly give away."

"Um, I'm not currently in the market."

"I can give you a good deal on them. They have a few flaws, but nothing you couldn't learn to live with."

"I'll let you know the minute I change my mind. But what I really want to know is how you got into arson investigation."

She held up a finger as she popped a roasted Brussel sprout into her mouth and chewed. I sipped a spoonful of soup, then reached for the bread and butter. In a moment she said, "It's a pretty long story. Actually, it's one of those intergenerational sagas."

"Excellent." I beamed at her. "I love a good story. And long is fine. After all, this bowl holds about a gallon of excellent soup, and there is a rumor about passionfruit meringues for after."

She shrugged. "Okay, you asked for it." And she reached for the basket of bread.

3

Bread buttered, and another bite of salad devoured, Penny sat back in her chair.

"Once upon a time," she began obediently, then stopped. "I don't think this is a whole story. I mean, it doesn't have an end."

"That's okay, it's still a story. You can bring it up to the present and end with something about pumpkin and Brussel sprouts."

She gave me a "you're crazy but I kind of like you" look and shrugged. "Okay, if you say so. Once upon a time there was a family of detectives."

"That's good," I encouraged.

"The grandpa detective was a captain on the San Francisco police force back in the Fifties. Man, did he have some tales to tell. Organized crime battles that went back to Prohibition times, bombings, murders. Okay, sorry, getting off track. Grandpa Detective left the force when he was thirty-five and started his own detective agency. He was good at it, and smart enough to marry a girl with a head for business. So before you know it, the detective agency has eight operatives, and the grandma and grandpa detectives have six children."

"Six kids? Sounds like they left the night surveillance to the eight operatives," I commented.

She chuckled. "It does at that. Of course they were Catholic and it was the Baby Boom, there were lots of big families back then. The six children grew up, and four of them went to work for the detective agency. The other two, the oldest boys, became firemen, and one of them trained to be an arson investigator for the Oakland fire department. All six of that generation had at least two kids, who now range in age from nineteen to forty seven."

"That span is a story unto itself. How many total grandkids for the grandma and grandpa detectives?"

"Seventeen."

"And you are one of the seventeen?"

"Yup. Right in the middle of the pack."

"I see what you mean about having lots of relatives. I confess there are times my one cousin feels like seventeen people though. She can be... formidable."

"Well, I'd still be happy to supplement her for you with some of mine. Anyway, all seventeen of us grew up hanging out at the detective agency. When we were little, they took us along on nighttime stakeouts. Grandpa drank coffee from a Thermos and read storybooks to us until we fell asleep in the back seat of the car. When we got older, other kids we knew had latchkeys and stayed alone until their parents got home from work, or maybe went to their grandparents' or a babysitter's house after school. We did our homework in the back room at the agency. There was a big case going on the night of my junior prom, and my date had to pick me up there. I thought it was *so* embarrassing, but then I found out he was bragging to everyone about it. I decided he didn't really like me, he just thought the detective thing was cool so I broke up with him."

"Oh, the scars we bear from youth."

"I know, right?" She laughed. "But we get over it. Don't ask me the guy's name. I can't remember it."

"So are you the offspring of a detective or a fireman?"

"Fireman. My dad was the arson investigator for Oakland. He retired ten, no, twelve years ago after a thirty-seven-year career."

"I bet he's got stories too."

"You should come to one of our Sunday dinners. It'll turn your hair white."

I thought about the liberal amount of gray already present on my head. "That wouldn't actually take much."

"My twin brother and I grew up with arson. We both always knew that's what we'd do. About five years ago he decided to get a dog to help him. He found this place in Arizona where you can either buy one of their dogs, or bring your own for training. So for a year before he got his dog, he researched and studied and searched for the perfect arson dog. He had charts, for goodness sake. He went to seminars. Just went totally overboard. I finally got sick of it all, so I told him I wanted to use an arson dog too. I signed up for the same session of the training course as him. Then I told him I was going to the pound to pick out a dog the day before our seminar started, and we'd see who had the better dog.

"So that's what I did. Went to the city pound, and walked up and down those cages with all those barking dogs. God, doesn't it just break your heart?"

I nodded, pressing my lips together tightly.

"Yeah, I see you get it. I wanted to take them all, every single barking dog in the place, and I couldn't. But finally I came to a cage with two dogs in it. One of them was a big black Lab, barking his head off, poor baby. And sitting quietly beside him was Daphne. She just looked at me, then she reached through the chain link with one paw."

"I'd have been a total goner," I confessed.

"Oh yeah," she nodded. "If they could teach all the dogs to do that paw thing the adoption rate would go up about a thousand percent. So that was it, I adopted her and we flew off to Arizona for arson detection school. And they almost wouldn't let us in. They'd never had a dog her size before come for training, and she was the only one in the class who wasn't a Lab or a Golden retriever. I thought my brother was going to fall down on the ground laughing when he saw her."

"Bet she showed him."

Penny grinned. "Big time. Don't get me wrong, his dog Flash is good, but Daphne was just born to do this work. She learned so fast that some jerk started a rumor that she'd been through the training before. Of course, they had to shut up when everyone on the course was sent the article from the shelter's support group about how—and when—she'd found her forever home. One of the advantages to having a unique dog is that no one could claim the picture was just a lookalike."

"I wonder if she did have any siblings. Do you constantly watch for similar ears?"

"I do! Haven't found any yet, but maybe someday. Anyway, since she joined the agency she's put over forty arsonists in jail."

"Wow." I looked down at Emily Ann and Jack. "Did you guys hear that? Daphne is the scourge of arsonists everywhere. You should get her autograph."

"No problem!" Penny reached into her leopard print purse and pulled out a business card. "P. W. Marquette, Arson Investigator, Marquette Detective Agency" was printed on one side with phone and email. "Turn it over," she said. I obeyed. On the back was a paw print with "Daphne" written under it.

I smiled and tucked the card into my pocket. "We're thrilled," I said. "This is our first souvenir from our trip. Well, except for the rock Jack made me pick up in Montana. It's shaped like a rabbit. He said it has special meaning for him."

4

We paused outside the restaurant, and I looked up and down the street. "This looks like a fun shopping district," I commented.

"Oh, it is. I love to window shop on my way home. You said you're staying with a friend? Where, exactly? I mean, what street?"

"Bob just moved into a little house on Acorn Street. Which I'm hoping you can tell me how to get back to or I'll have to get out my GPS."

"I don't believe this! *I* live on Acorn. Is Bob tall, a little gray at the temples?"

"That's him."

"Then we're neighbors. I'm across the street and two houses down from his."

"Cool, then you should be able to give me directions. What luck."

"I'm actually on my way home. Want to walk together or do you have errands?"

"That would be great. Can we do some of that window shopping on the way?"

"You bet. Come on, Daphne, this way." She looked down at her dog and added, "And no more squirrels, do you hear?"

"Same goes for you guys," I told Emily Ann and Jack. He wagged agreeably, but Emily Ann turned her head away. I think she rolled her eyes like a twelve-year-old girl.

The shopping district was about three blocks long, a mix of services for the surrounding neighborhood, several eateries, and some upscale shops. The dry cleaner, insurance agency, print shop and hair salon could be passed quickly. There was a shoe repair place, scarcely wider than the entry door, that had a display of antique shoes I knew would interest Kay, as would the shop with the midcentury furniture and accessories in the window. Emily Ann peered longingly into the pet store, but I told her we were just window shopping today and would come back later.

We strolled past a toy store and a shop with hand printed Indian textiles, chatting idly about some of the items in the windows. Next to that we passed a place called "The Inward Horizon." A beautifully calligraphed sign promised

Books, Talismans & Herbs
Life Readings by Madame Nora

The Dutch door to the shop was painted a deep blue, and the top half was open invitingly. I glanced in. The space looked shaded and cool. An inviting smell of herbs wafted our way.

Penny said, "This next place is kind of fun. It's a portrait photographer that's been here forever. I think they opened right after World War Two. There's always a display of their past work and it's interesting to see how hairstyles and clothes change through the decades."

We left the psychic's shop and paused by the photographer's. The current display in the window was a collection of portraits from the Fifties. The centerpiece was a large, hand-colored photograph of a bride posed before an ornate church alter, her satin train carefully arranged to flow down four carpeted steps. Enormous floral arrangements bracketed her on each side. Behind the altar a full length portrait of Jesus gazed down at her.

"Wow, what a dress," Penny said, staring at the picture. "I always wonder how they can walk in those things."

"Yeah, me too. My mother made me wear a dress with a train when I got married and I tripped on the damned thing on the way to the alter."

"Really? You didn't actually fall down, did you?"

"No, just tripped enough to appear completely clumsy. Actually, I tripped once on the way down, and once on the way back." I paused. "Too bad I didn't realize on the way down that tripping was an omen. I should have picked up that train and run like hell."

Penny looked down at me with a half-smile. "I'll have to take you out for a drink in a few days and get the whole story from you."

"Not much to tell," I shrugged. "Bad choice. Over now. Who else is in this window?"

Penny pointed at a black and white photo of a girl, about ten years old, plaid bows on her pigtails, grinning straight at the camera. "She looks like fun."

"I'll say. Maybe we can find her and bring her along for that drink."

"Good idea."

My eyes traveled on, lingering over family groups and infants in christening gowns with kewpie doll curls on top of their head. At last I noticed the picture on a stand in the corner of the display window, and the world around me faded into nonexistence.

A studio portrait of a young woman and a little girl old enough to sit up, but probably not walking yet. Every detail of their clothing and hair and jewelry were period perfect, but it was the woman's face that held me. All the sounds around me were silenced as I gazed into what could be a mirror. But a mirror in time, because she looked just like I looked in my twenties.

I focused on the child snuggled into the curve of the woman's arm, and I caught my breath. Babies pretty much all look alike to me, and many have chubby cheeks and blond curls.

But this one was wearing a little dress of a distinctive plaid, with smocked Scotties across the bodice and more dancing around the hem of the skirt.

My peripheral vision dimmed, and all I could see was the baby's dress.

I still owned that dress. I'd had it framed in a shadow box a couple of years earlier, and hung it on the wall of my bedroom. Inside it was a hand-embroidered tag that read "Made with love for little Louisa."

Oakland, California

Midcentury

Eloise Chessman pulled the taffeta skirt close so that she could close the car door. Her glasses steamed over. She took them off and looked around for something to wipe them with as she rolled the window down a crack. Louisa's diaper bag was sitting on the floor in front of the passenger seat, so she leaned over and fished out a clean diaper and wiped her glasses with a corner of the soft cotton square.

"There, see, you're a very handy person to have around," she said to the baby. Louisa bounced in her car seat beside Eloise and gurgled at her mother. "Maybe by the time you're grown up they'll invent glasses that don't fog up or get smeary. Wouldn't that be wonderful?"

She tucked the diaper back into the bag, then straightened and put her hands on the steering wheel. Her feet reached for the pedals. "Oh, phooey," she said. "I can't drive in these high heels. Why didn't you remind me before we got in the car?" She slipped off her shoes and nudged them over by the diaper bag. "Okay, here we go. Let's go see Daddy and have our picture made."

Louisa bounced again and banged on her seat with her fist.

Eloise pushed in the clutch and turned on the ignition. The Chevy's engine turned over and caught, and she released the emergency brake pedal with her stockinged foot. She backed carefully out of the driveway and drove down the hill. The midmorning traffic was light, and she was in good time. Too good— she was early for her appointment, as she often was.

The last traffic light turned yellow as she approached, and she braked to a stop. Glancing in the mirror to check her lipstick, she noticed the color of the car two cars back. That dark blue was the color her father had ordered for the car her husband used for work. "Image is part of everything you wear or use or say," her father always maintained, "and image is a big part of your credibility."

The light turned green, and the car behind Eloise tooted its horn before she could get started again. "Honestly," she muttered to the baby beside her. "What's their big hurry?" She pulled the gear shift into first and let in the clutch. Midway down the next block she turned on her left turn signal to pull into the photographer's parking lot. As she turned, she glanced in her mirror again, expecting to see the dark blue car follow her. Instead it swept on down the street. Two people were in the car, a man and a woman. He gave an impression of broad shoulders in a dark suit, wearing a gray hat pulled low over his eyes. The glimpse she got of the woman was of someone small and dark.

Eloise's brow knit in puzzlement. Surely that had been Carter, though he didn't usually wear a hat. But who was he with, and where was he going? Their appointment for a portrait with little Louisa was in just a few minutes. Perhaps the woman was a customer, and he was dropping her off somewhere before coming to the studio.

She hoped he wouldn't be long. Keeping a six-month-old baby clean for any length of time was challenging, not to mention staying neat herself. She knew how sticky baby hands could wrinkle a dress, and Louisa was fascinated with her mother's rhinestone buttons. She thought they looked good enough to eat and tried to do so at any opportunity.

"But maybe it wasn't your daddy after all," Eloise said aloud to the baby. Louisa looked at her with a wise expression. "Okay, let's go on in and get you ready, and when Daddy comes we won't keep him waiting." Carter was often impatient with her. Still, she preferred that treatment to its flip side, when he turned indifferent. His coldness shriveled her. He would hate waiting while she fussed with Louisa's hair or dress.

Two blocks away, Carter Chessman eased the heavy Buick into a parking place at the curb and shifted the gear into neutral. "I have to go," he said to the woman beside him. "Her father made this appointment for a damned portrait. Got to prove we're a happy little family."

The woman pulled the fur collar of her coat close around her neck and glanced sideways at him. "Well, darling, you would go and get her pregnant." Her voice was amused, but the amusement did not reach her dark eyes.

"Oh, god, not that again," he groaned. "How many times do I have to apologize? Just tell me and I'll apologize that many times and we'll be done with it."

"Better her than me," she sniffed. "Will I see you tonight?"

He nodded. "Sure, but it may be pretty late. Her family is coming to dinner."

She gave him a cold look before she slid toward the passenger door and put a hand on the door. "Don't bother. I may be out."

He reached over and closed a large hand around her arm. "What, you're stepping out on me?" he asked, and pulled her back toward him. He bent his head to kiss her. "You know there's no one for you but me. It won't be much longer."

She turned her face aside and pulled her arm from his grasp. "It had better not be. I didn't mind sharing you for a little while, but this is getting ridiculous. And now you have a baby as well. I know the job and the wife were a package deal, but I am getting well and truly fed up." She opened the door, stepped out of the car and walked away down the street, her hips making the folds of the calf-length trapeze coat sway with every step. He frowned as he watched her until she had disappeared around a corner, then reached into his pocket for a pack of cigarettes.

He pushed in the lighter on the dashboard, and when it clicked out a few moments later used it to light his cigarette. Blowing smoke toward the ceiling without taking the white tube from his mouth, he replaced the lighter. He was getting fed up with the situation himself. He'd never expected it to go on for so long. Eloise getting pregnant had complicated everything. On the one hand, his father-in-law—and boss—was delighted. But he had hoped to move his plan forward months before now, and the time had never been right.

He briefly toyed with the idea of abandoning everything and just walking away. But no; Eloise's father would hunt him down with all the considerable resources at his disposal. And they were so close to being ready. A few more details in place, and he and Joan would be set for life.

He'd been careful never to tell anyone here where he was really from; they thought he came from the Boston area. He'd borrowed a new name. Its former owner had died in Korea and wouldn't miss it. If everything went according to plan they would be out of here and have the whole world to choose from for a place to settle. And if something went wrong, well, he could disappear back to Willow Falls and be safe.

If he cut and ran now, he wouldn't have the money. And there was no guarantee that Joan would go with him without it.

He put the Buick into gear and looked over his shoulder before pulling back onto the street in a U-turn. The photographer's studio was a couple of blocks back. Better get this damned picture-taking over with.

5

"Louisa? Louisa. Hey, Louisa?"

The voice reached me dimly, as though from far away. I blinked and looked around. The street was unfamiliar, and the woman saying my name a stranger. I felt the touch of a cold dog nose on my hand, and took a deep breath. And recognized Penny, and that the street was in Berkeley, and that I was standing in front of a photographer's shop.

With a picture in the window that I could not explain.

"Louisa," Penny said again. "Are you okay?"

"Yes. Yes, of course, I'm fine."

"I thought you were going to faint. Or that you were having a heart attack or something."

"Sorry. I don't know what came over me. It was just..." I looked down. Jack and Emily Ann were both gazing at me with worried faces. "Hey, I'm fine, everyone. That picture just made me—I didn't know who—"

"Here." Penny took my arm and led me and the dogs to a nearby bus shelter. She gave me a gentle push, and I sat on the bench. "You look like you've seen a ghost."

"I—I'm not sure what I saw. But you may be right. I may have seen a ghost."

I was on the phone with Kay later that afternoon when Bob got home. I mouthed the word 'Kay' as I sketched a little wave at him. "Bob just got home," I told her.

"Let me talk to him," she demanded.

In chorus Bob said, "Let me talk to her."

I stepped close and gave him a quick kiss on the mouth, then handed over my phone.

"Kay! How are you! ... It sure is...I know, I can hardly believe she's here. I bet you miss her...You are absolutely right, I labored under a weight of guilt all day. I thought I could rearrange appointments but it was impossible...well, the colleague who was going to cover for me had a baby last night. It was three weeks overdue and I don't think she was willing to postpone the birth for one more day, so I had to step up to the plate...I promise I will, although you may have noticed that Louisa does appreciate a bit of time to herself...And how is Ed these days? Are you guys on again or off again?...Oh, that's good. Tell him I said hi...I will...Okay, here's Louisa."

He handed back the phone. "Stop grinning," I told him before putting it to my ear. "Okay, so you can send me that stuff tomorrow?"

32

"I'll get everything ready tonight and send it by overnight mail first thing tomorrow," she promised. "Do you want the actual photographs, or would it be just as good if I scanned them and sent them in an email?"

"Hmmm. Maybe…how about both. Scan and email, then stick the originals in the box with the dress."

"No problem."

"I sure wish your mom was still with us. I—I would really like to ask her some questions."

"So would I. So would I."

We said our farewells and I flipped the phone closed, sticking it in my jeans pocket. "Hey, you're home," I said to Bob.

He had settled on the sofa with a dog on either side of him. Jack had rolled onto his back for a tummy scratch, and Emily Ann rested her head on his knee. He looked up with a smile. "This is awfully nice to come home to."

I sat down on the other side of Emily Ann. It was actually more of a perch, since she took up so much of the sofa. "And we're all mighty glad to see you." I leaned across the dog to give him a kiss. "How was your day?"

"Surprisingly productive. One of the private clients had a breakthrough with an issue he's been stuck on for weeks. And we solved an editing problem at the studio, so the new interview is almost ready to broadcast."

Bob is a hypnotherapist and had been invited to participate in a research project at the university.

"Wonderful. Sounds like you had a good day."

"I still feel bad about going off and leaving you on your first day here. I had all sorts of plans."

"Oh, pooh. We can do stuff together tomorrow or the next day. And as you so rightly observed to my cousin, that Louisa does like time to herself."

"Are you hungry? Want to go out?"

"I'm not starving yet, but sure, whenever."

"What did you end up doing today?"

"Well...I met one of your neighbors, and we had lunch, and—and then we found something, um, odd."

"Odd? Well, it *is* Berkeley after all. Some of my neighbors are bound to be odd."

"Oh, Penny's not odd. She's quite cool, actually."

"Which neighbor is she?"

"Across the street and two houses down. The house with the white picket fence and the roses."

"Tall? Interesting taste in clothes? Small dog?"

"That's the one. She's an arson investigator and—"

"Arson! Seriously?"

I nodded. "Seriously. And that little dog is her arson dog. Daphne. She said Daphne has put something like forty arsonists away."

"I had no idea there was so much arson in the area."

"Oh, she gets called in all over the country. They just got back from, um, I think it was Minneapolis. Someone torched a car dealership."

"Huh. I bet she's got some great stories."

34

"Mmm hmmm. You'll like her. But it was after lunch that we found, um, I saw…" I wasn't sure how to go on.

"Found what?" His expression was interested and encouraging, but I found it hard to describe what I'd seen.

"Well, it's—oh heck, just let me show you. It's a picture. Down in that shopping district at the bottom of the hill."

He brightened. "Great. I was going to suggest we walk down there for dinner."

"Oh, good. I mean, I had lunch with Penny at this place with a patio for the dogs, and the food was fabulous."

"Was it Mintie's?"

"Yup, sure was. You've been there?"

"Several times. It reminds me of the Bluebird."

"Me too! No wonder you like this neighborhood."

"Actually, it's probably way too tempting living so close to them. A couple of the other places down there are excellent as well."

"That's pretty much what Penny said. Of course, it's not like we don't eat at the Bluebird all the time."

"True. But only the Bluebird Cafe has Cleta."

"Stop, you're making me feel homesick."

"I'm making myself feel homesick. All right, let me go wash up, and we'll go out for dinner and an evening stroll. And to see your picture."

"Shall we take the dogs? I should probably feed them first in any case."

"Of course let's take them. Want to go to Mintie's again? Or we could try the Middle Eastern place, they have a patio too."

"Mintie's is good. I have an ambition to eat my way through their entire menu."

He stood and smiled down at me. "I like that. They change the menu all the time, so you may have to stay here forever to try everything."

I postponed showing Bob the photographer's window display until after dinner. I was glad to have a different waiter; it seemed a little embarrassing to show up at the same restaurant twice in one day. Of course, we do that at the Bluebird all the time, so I'm not sure what the difference is—a sense of home, perhaps. In any case, the food was still wonderful, and the dogs were thrilled with their plates of treats.

The sun was low on the horizon when we left the restaurant, We strolled through the lengthening shadows up the street, past the midcentury furniture, the pet shop, the toy store, the life readings place, and on to the photography studio. Subtle lighting had been turned on in the window display, and each vintage picture glowed.

"Just take a look at the pictures in this window. I want to see if you, um, if you notice the same thing I did."

"Do I win anything if I do?" Bob's grin was mischievous.

"I'll have a scrumptious dog treat ready for you as soon as we get home. Or I might even share a bite of what's left of my dessert." I waved the small white box under his nose.

"Mmmm, hard choice. Okay, let me look."

Bob has wonderful powers of concentration. He handed me Jack's leash and clasped his hands behind his back and began to study each picture in turn. The bride, the family groups, the infants, the girl with the pigtails. Then he arrived at the picture in the far corner. He looked it over, started to look away, and then his eyes returned to the young woman holding the baby. He leaned over to get as close as possible to the window. His brows pulled together as he stared for a long time. At last he stirred.

"Unbelievable," he breathed out, almost as a sigh. He turned his head sideways to look at me. "You didn't have them Photoshop this or something, did you? A test to see if I'm worthy of that dessert?"

"Can they do that?"

"I think so. All things seem possible with digital images these days. Did you?"

"Of course not! Why would I do that? I mean, why would anyone do something like that? No."

He straightened. "Didn't think so, I was merely grasping at straws. The alternative is that this picture looks just like you."

"Quite a bit younger."

"Just like you."

"Like I did at that age. But it gets weirder." I peered in the window, studying the picture once more.

"Weirder how? Seeing your double isn't weird enough?"

37

"See the dress the baby is wearing?"

He turned back to the window. "Okay. What about it?"

"Does it ring any bells?"

He studied the picture with a frown. "No, I don't...oh, wait a minute. Where have I seen something like that?"

I kept silent, giving him time to think.

"Got it! That framed piece on your wall. In the bedroom. A little dress. Is it like this one?"

"Bingo."

"But—it's just a coincidence. Right? I mean, it was a cute little dress from, er, Sears or someplace like that. Probably a zillion baby girls wore them that year."

"*That* one might be a mass produced piece from Sears, I don't know yet. But the one on my wall, no."

"Are you sure?"

I regarded him with amusement. "Bob, recall how I spend my time and who I hang out with when I am not at the dog park. Antique store? Cousin who knows everything about antiques?"

"Rings a bell, yes."

"I may not do needlework myself, but I recognize the real thing when I see it. I framed that little dress because it is a work of art, just as much as if it were paint on canvas. Every stitch was done by hand, not just the smocking but all of the seams, the buttonholes, everything."

"Wow."

"The smocking alone would have taken hours and hours of work. And there is a hand-stitched label inside saying it was made for Louisa."

"Okay. Not from Sears."

"You'll be able to see for yourself when it gets here."

"The dress?"

"Yes. That's what I was talking to Kay about when you got home this afternoon."

"Oh, right. Cool."

"She's overnighting it, along with some family pictures. What's today? Wednesday? I'll call this studio tomorrow and make an appointment for Friday."

"Good idea. I wonder who the people in the picture are. Maybe she's your aunt or something. Did your parents bring you on a trip to California when you were a baby?"

I stared at him. "What? No. Oh, good grief, I've never told you this, have I? I was born here. In Oakland."

"Really? I always thought you were born in Willow Falls."

"Nope, right here. There's probably a Louisa Chelton Memorial Birthplace plaque at the hospital. We'll have to look for it if we have time."

Bob chuckled. "We'll do that. And find out who's in this picture. Wow. What a coincidence. Maybe you'll find a whole new bunch of cousins you never knew you had."

I handed back Jack's leash, and we turned to head back up the hill to Bob's house. "That would be fun. Though it would feel really odd to have more than just Kay. It seems wrong to, I don't know, dilute her."

He laughed and caught my free hand with his. "Louisa, absolutely nothing on earth could dilute Kay."

6

Oakland, California

Midcentury

"So when am I going to have a picture of my girls?" Frank Abernathy demanded as he broke a hunk of bread off the crusty loaf and smeared butter on it.

"Only two of your girls, Daddy. Don't forget about Lennie," Eloise said, smiling across the table at her younger sister. The fifteen-year-old was scowling down at her plate and didn't acknowledge her sister's attempt to include her.

Their father snorted in dismissal. "I sometimes wish I could forget about Lennie," he said curtly. He twirled spaghetti expertly onto the fork and into his mouth. A moment of silence stretched into awkwardness.

"We should be able to see the proofs on Wednesday," Carter finally said. "I think we got a few good shots before Louisa started fussing. We should have taken Lennie instead." He gave his young sister-in-law a private smile and a wink, and the girl's cheeks grew pink.

Eloise paused in buttering her own bread. "Darling! Louisa was as good as gold! She was an angel until they fussed so long with the lights and she got hungry. Nathan said he'd never seen such a good baby."

Frank said, "Who the hell is Nathan?"

"Nathan Gallagher. You remember, we went to high school together."

Her father frowned and shook his head.

"We both were on the staff of the school paper. Anyway, his dad owns the photography studio, and Nate works there now."

Carter frowned at her and she fell silent. He turned to her father and said, "How did your meeting go this afternoon, sir? Any likelihood of their business?"

Frank took a sip of wine before he answered. "It looks promising, my boy. We're playing golf with them tomorrow afternoon, and I want you to play a very careful game. Keep just ahead until the last couple of holes and then let them beat you."

Carter nodded. "I can do that. Drinks at the club afterward?"

"Oh yes," the older man nodded. "Drinks and business, and they'll be in the mood to buy. If we get this account we'll be in the big leagues. Just think of it. Bank of America's brand new magnetic printing technology. That ink coming out of my plant is going to be black gold."

"Honestly," Eloise put in. "Why all the subterfuge? If you've got what they want, why not just make a deal?"

Both her husband and her father looked at her contemptuously. Her sister spoke up. "Oh, Ely, it's not that easy. Carter knows what he's doing."

Carter laughed. "That's right, I know what I'm doing. You listen to your little sister. She's obviously the smart one in the family." He turned back to his father-in-law and made a remark in a low voice. Both men laughed.

Lennie blushed again and dropped her eyes to her plate, but she couldn't hide her smile. Eloise sat back in her chair and looked from her husband to her sister and back again. Her jaw tightened.

Just then she heard the sound that always caused an instant reaction. Louisa, upstairs in her crib, began to cry. Eloise felt the familiar tightening in her chest, as though there were still a physical connection between her and her child. She pushed back her chair and started to rise.

"Sit down," snapped Carter. "It won't hurt Louisa to cry herself back to sleep for once. You spoil her."

Eloise hesitated, then continued to stand. "I'll only be a moment," she said. "If she's really awake I'll bring her down. Daddy hasn't seen her yet this evening.

Lennie, it looks like Daddy could use some more spaghetti."

"That's right, bring her down and let me spoil her," Frank said.

Ten minutes later Eloise reappeared, carrying Louisa on her hip.

"What took you so long?" Carter said irritably. He and Frank had both lit up cigarettes and a blue haze hung between them. When Louisa heard his voice she turned her face and pressed it against her mother's neck. Eloise reached up and smoothed back a damp curl.

"I didn't think you wanted me to bring her down with a wet diaper," she replied evenly.

"I didn't want you to bring her down at all."

"Nonsense," interjected Frank. "Let me hold her. Come see Grandpa." He pushed his chair back a few inches, shifted the cigarette he was holding to his lips and patted his lap. Eloise walked closer to him and tried to shift the baby, but Louisa clung tighter to her mother.

"It's okay, sweetie," Eloise said, patting Louisa's back. "Grandpa wants to see you." She loosened Louisa's grip and swung her down to Frank's lap. Lennie put out a hand as though to stop her, but then dropped it and turned her head away. Louisa wrinkled her face, trying to decide whether to cry, but her grandfather tickled her tummy and she smiled instead.

"There's my girl!" the older man crowed. He bounced his knee up and down, and Louisa gurgled.

Eloise watched the two of them for a moment, then said, "I'll go get dessert while you play with Louisa. Lennie, could you help me clear the plates?"

Lennie scowled, but she pushed back her chair and stood. She gathered dirty plates and used silverware, then pushed through the door to the kitchen, letting it swing back into Eloise's face. Eloise blocked it with her shoulder and managed to keep her handful of wine glasses from being smashed.

"Thanks a lot," Eloise said to her sister when she'd followed her into the kitchen.

"You're welcome," Lennie replied in her most sarcastic tone. She set down her load of plates beside the sink and reached into her pocket, pulling out a crumpled package of cigarettes. She took one, replaced the packet, and turned on one of the gas burners of the stove to light it.

"I wish you wouldn't smoke," Eloise said, frowning at her younger sister. "It looks so trashy."

"Maybe I am trashy," Lennie growled. "You obviously got all the classy genes in the family. I'm just the leftover."

"Lennie! Don't talk that way. There's nothing genetic about whether you choose to smoke or not." Eloise set the wine glasses down by the plates Lennie had brought through. "There's a bowl of whipped cream in the fridge. Could you get that out while I slice this cake?"

Lennie tapped ash onto the kitchen floor, shrugged, and turned toward the refrigerator. Before she could open the door, noise erupted from the dining room. Baby cries mixed with a man's shout. Both women froze in place, then Eloise was through the swinging door into the dining room.

Louisa was red-faced, her eyes screwed shut as she wailed. Frank was dabbing at her arm with a wet napkin, but she wouldn't hold still. Carter had pushed his chair away from the table and was rubbing his pants leg with a napkin, a furious scowl on his face.

Eloise's first thought was that her father was about to drop the flailing baby. She leapt forward and took the screaming child into her arms. "What is going on?" She had to raise her voice to be heard over Louisa's cries. She rubbed the baby's back and rocked her back and forth, and the cries started to subside.

Her father looked abashed, but Carter was plainly furious. "Your kid kicked the water pitcher over."

"The water pitcher! How could she even reach it?"

"It was my fault," Frank admitted. "We were playing airplane and I was holding her up and flying her around, and she kicked and the pitcher went over and got Carter wet."

"But why is she crying like this?"

Frank looked down, unable to meet her eyes. "When I reached for a napkin for Carter, some cigarette ash fell on Louisa's arm."

Eloise looked down and saw an angry red spot just above Louisa's left wrist. "You burned my baby?" she said incredulously, her arms tightening around the child.

"She'll be all right," Frank said gruffly.

"I cannot believe you burned her with your stupid cigarettes. Don't you have any sense?" Fury rose in her throat.

Carter stood up. "I have to change out of these wet slacks," he said, and left the room. In a moment they heard his footsteps going up the stairs.

Frank stood as well. "We'd better go. Lennie, come on, we're going home," he called He turned and walked through the living room to the closet by the front door, where he retrieved his overcoat. As he shrugged into the sleeves, he frowned and barked loudly, "Lennie!"

At his shout, Louisa began to wail again. Eloise rocked her in her arms. "There, there, sweetie, you're okay, I've got you," she murmured.

The door from the kitchen swung open, and Lennie came through. As she slouched through the living room, she said, "I thought we were going to have dessert."

"Not tonight," Frank barked. "Let's go." He reached for the door.

"Don't you have a coat?" Eloise asked her sister.

"It's not cold," Lennie mumbled, and stepped out into the night. Her father followed her without another word to Eloise. Lennie paused on the porch steps and looked back. "Listen," she said, "um, be careful, okay?"

Eloise went to her and gave her a quick hug. "Hey, I'm not the one who's careless with cigarettes around here. We'll be fine."

47

She watched them climb into the dark blue Cadillac at the curb. The engine roared to life, the lights came on, and they were gone.

Louisa's crying began to subside, and she laid her head on her mother's shoulder. Eloise could tell she was about ready to go back to sleep. She went back into the house, closed the front door and patted the child's back as she went back to the kitchen. There she found that her sister had left her burning cigarette balanced on the edge of the kitchen table. A pile of ash was on the floor, and the still-glowing tip was resting on a charred spot on the table's wooden top. She bit off an exclamation, picked up the butt, and threw it into the sink.

Her shoulders sagged as she looked around the jumbled room, at the dirty dishes stacked haphazardly in the sink and the pans she'd used to cook still on the stove. She had hoped her sister would help with the dishes.

"And instead she's trying to burn down the house," she said out loud. Louisa stirred in her arms. "Come on, let's settle you first. Maybe a miracle will happen and your daddy will dry the dishes."

As she headed for the stairs, she heard footsteps descending and looked up. Her husband had changed clothes completely. He went past her to the hall closet and opened it, pulling out a short jacket.

"Where are you going?" she asked in surprise.

"I need to check something at the office," he said, not looking at her. "I'm not sure how long I'll be. Don't wait up."

48

"But—"

"I said don't wait up! I just need some air. I've had enough baby noise for one night." He opened the front door and stepped out, pulling it shut behind him.

Eloise sank down onto the third step and settled Louisa on her lap. Two slow tears seeped down her cheeks. The baby looked at her mother's face and reached up to touch one of the tears with her index finger. Eloise looked at her daughter and gave her a tremulous smile.

"Don't you worry, my sweet Louisa," she said. "Everything will be all right. I love you enough for two people."

7

I had enjoyed Penny and Daphne so much that I called her the next day. Since the number I had was the one on the business card she had given me, it was no surprise when she answered on the second ring.

"Good morning, Marquette Detective Agency."

"Penny? It's Louisa McGuire."

"Louisa! Hi! I was just thinking about you."

"Oh, um, good. Then I don't need to remind you who I am."

"Of course not. I never forget anyone who saves my dog's life. What can I do for you?"

"I wondered if you might be able to join us for breakfast Friday morning at Bob's house. I promised to make him my famous croissant French toast."

"Wow, yum. You bet. My schedule is wide open Friday morning."

"Wonderful. Tell me if there's anything you can't eat or don't like."

"I hate mushrooms and kale. Other than that I'm wide open for all culinary adventure."

"Then we're golden, because while I sometimes do interesting variations, my French toast never includes mushrooms or kale."

"Yeah, kale French toast. Sounds like the kind of thing you'd serve your worst enemy. So, what time, and what can I bring?"

"Ten o'clock, and just bring Daphne to play with Emily Ann and Jack."

"I can handle that. See you tomorrow, and thanks!"

Penny and Bob were talking like lifelong friends by the time I slid their plates of French toast in front of them. She had brought a pitcher of fresh squeezed orange juice and a lovely bottle of champagne, and the resulting mimosas made breakfast feel like a party. Penny's floral shirtwaist dress added to the garden-party ambiance.

We settled on the terrace under the vine-covered pergola in Bob's back yard. Daphne entertained us by leading the bigger dogs in a spirited romp. Bob picked up his glass and held it high.

"Here's to Louisa, for a magnificent breakfast," he toasted.

"Here, here!" Penny chanted gaily, and we all clinked glasses. "This looks just wonderful. Are you sure you have to go back to that little town? I think you should stay here and feed me things like this on a regular basis."

"That's what I keep saying," Bob added.

They both smiled at me warmly.

Did I love Bob enough to stay here? I had missed him since he'd moved to California...but did I miss him enough? I wanted to wail, "I don't know what to do-o-o!" I took a breath.

"I had forgotten how beautiful it is here, especially this time of year," I finally managed.

The doorbell rang, and all three dogs charged into the house, barking. Bob rose. "I'll get it. Maybe it's your package."

Penny and I tried the food. "Mmmm, this is great," she said. "Love the sliced almonds on it."

"Thanks. I spent a few days last winter minding a bed and breakfast, and it was a real hit with the guests." One of whom had proved to be a counterfeiter who nearly succeeded in turning a nearby deserted house into my tomb, but that didn't need to come into the conversation.

Bob returned with a small box. He had paused in the kitchen to slice open the formidable amount of heavy tape in which Kay envelopes any package she ships.

"Here you go," he said, placing it on the table by my plate.

I lifted a flap and peeked inside. "Oh, good, she sent everything. Let's look at it after breakfast. Kay will kill me if I get maple syrup on the family album. Which I know I would." To Penny I said, "I asked my cousin to send me some stuff. I'll show you if it won't bore you."

"Can't wait," she said, and took another bite.

When everyone was finished we cleared the table and stacked the dishes in the dishwasher. Bob made quick work of cleaning the electric griddle, and Penny and I poured out new mimosas. Returning to the terrace, we settled at the table once more. The dogs lay in the shade of the oak tree, though Daphne's enormous ears remained on the alert.

I pulled an extra chair closer and set Kay's box on it, then lifted the flaps. On top of a tissue wrapped item was a note.

"Call me as soon as you get this! I've included the album that you asked for, and I also stuck in one of my parents' albums. Hadn't looked at it for ages! What a blast from the past! Now—CALL me!"

"Hang on a sec," I said to the others. "This note says I'm supposed to call her immediately to let her know it arrived." I pulled my phone out of my jeans pocket and tapped in her number. It rang several times, then the standard recorded voice came on to tell me that my party was not currently available, and I could leave a message after the tone, and that I could hang up when I was finished or hold on for more options.

"Kay, it's Louisa. I hope you're not answering because you're in the middle of selling that enormous Victorian armoire for a zillion dollars. Just wanted to tell you the package arrived and we're about to dig in. Thanks a heap for sending it. I'll talk to you later."

Phone duty done, I returned to the box. Eagerly I pulled out the floppy tissue-wrapped item on top.

"Oh boy, presents!" Penny grinned.

"Sort of. I asked her to send me something from my house." I turned the piece over, intending to unstick the tape, but Kay had gone overboard again. The 3M Company must love her. I shrugged and tore the paper open, carefully unfolded the fabric within, lifted it from the tissue paper and gave it a little shake.

"Ohhh," breathed Penny, "that is adorable!"

I handed the little dress across the table to her and she held it up to inspect it. Autumn light filtered through the oak leaves onto the asymmetrical-plaid silk fabric that gleamed in jewel tones of rose, sage green, and amethyst.

"Gosh, look at this embroidery. I don't know anything about needlework, but all these tiny details are impressive." She carefully handed back the little dress. "Was this yours when you were a baby? Did your mom keep it tucked away with, I don't know, lavender sachets?"

"Something like that." I smiled at her, trying to make the smile look real, trying not to remember finding the dress in a box of cast offs in my parents' attic after they died. I'd almost thrown the box away without looking through it. The stuff on top was a mess of tangled yarn, an old hair brush, a pink princess phone with the rotary dial missing, some women's magazines from the Seventies. I had tipped the lot into a garbage bag, but a wad of cloth stuck in the bottom corner of the box. I'd picked at it gingerly, grabbed it delicately with thumb and forefinger, lifted it out and held it over the open mouth of the garbage bag.

Suspended in the air like that, the cloth had rolled open and I saw it was a little dress. The exquisite embroidery on the tiny bodice practically glowed against the colors of the fabric. I'd dropped the garbage bag and sank down on the floor, smoothing the fabric over my lap.

A full skirt belled out from the tightly gathered bodice, smocked with three motifs across the front—little black Scotty dogs facing out from a veritable garden of embroidered flowers. Roses of bullion stitch, delphiniums depicted in French knots, and more. The brown eyes of each dog sparkled with the tiniest dot of white. I almost expected them to blink at me. The Peter Pan collar and puffed sleeves were of a coordinated solid color fabric in amethyst that matched the color in the plaid, edged with bias piping of the main fabric. On each sleeve was another Scotty in its garden, and the collar was adorned with clusters of roses. More Scotties danced around the hem of the skirt. Even in its crumpled state it was clearly the work of expert hands.

As I stared at it, I had a niggling feeling I had seen it before, and somehow it was connected with Kay. Perhaps it had been one of her baby dresses and somehow had ended up at my parents' house? I picked it up again and turned it wrong-side-out to look at its construction, and noticed the hand-stitched lettering on the tag sewn into the waist.

Made with love

for little
Louisa

I felt a nudge at my knee. Jack was standing there and suddenly I was back at the table in Bob's back yard in Berkeley. Bob reached over and gently took the little dress from my hands. I picked up my neglected mimosa and took a sip.

"I know I've seen it before at your house, but I confess I never paid much attention to it."

"Of course not. You're a guy. It's a baby dress." My smile felt more real this time. I reached down and gave Jack a pat.

"I see what you mean about it being a work of art though." He peered at the embroidery. "How did they do such tiny stitches?"

Penny stirred on her chair. "Why do I get the feeling I've seen it before? May I?" She held out a hand and Bob gave her the dress to study.

"Remember the picture we saw yesterday, of the woman holding the baby?"

She looked up from her inspection of the Scotties, her eyes wide. "Oh. Right. The little girl was wearing something like this dress."

I nodded. "I—I've always wondered who made this. My mother didn't sew. She was...not very domestic. Anyway, I made an appointment at the photography studio for later today. I'm hoping they'll let me look at that picture more closely. Even if the dress isn't identical, who knows, maybe I'll get a clue."

Penny made a face. "Darn, I wish I didn't have this client meeting so I could go with you."

"I do too," said Bob, "but I've got a patient to see at three. We're all deserting you, Louisa."

I shook my head. "I think I'd rather go alone anyway."

"What time is your appointment again?" he asked.

"Three thirty."

"Good, that still gives you plenty of time to get ready before the party this evening."

"Party?" This was the first I'd heard of a party. It had better not be here.

"I'm sure I told you. At Erik Landisen's house. Just a little get-together with some of my colleagues."

"I don't remember you mentioning it." Did all men do this? So far, Bob had not been remotely like my dead husband Roger. However, not telling me something yet still expecting me to know about it had been one of Roger's favorite tactics.

"I'm sure I told you," Bob said again. Then, "I think I told you." His expression became stricken. "Maybe I just intended to tell you and forgot."

I laughed. "We've all done that. What time? What should I wear?"

"Seven thirty. Casual."

I nodded. What constituted evening casual in Berkeley? Had I brought anything appropriate along? I tried to think of what I had unpacked when I arrived. Jeans and casual shirts were all I could picture. Would I have to go shopping? Where?

Thank heavens I had met Penny, she could guide me.

I turned back to her, a little embarrassed that Bob and I had had this conversation in front of her. She was still poring over the dress.

"I'd love to get a closer look at that picture," she commented. "Maybe you could get a copy from them. I still can't believe how much the woman looked like you."

"Probably just coincidence," I maintained, "but I have to check it out. Just think, I might never have seen it if we hadn't gone window shopping after lunch."

"Which of course was all due to Daphne and the squirrel."

"Squirrel?" asked Bob. "What squirrel?"

8

A bell tinkled over the door when I entered the photography studio that afternoon. As well as my purse I carried a small canvas bag containing the baby dress and an envelope with a few snapshots I had removed from the albums Kay had sent.

The front part of the shop was small, perhaps twenty feet wide, with a large wooden leather-topped Eastlake desk a few paces back from the entry, and a seating area off to the right with a couple of slipper chairs and a small round table that held some photography magazines. A slatted wall behind the desk displayed a variety of portraits, all of more recent vintage than the display in the window. A door in the wall stood ajar, leading I assumed to their actual studio and work areas. As I hesitated by the door, a young man entered from the back and paused behind the desk.

"Hi!" he said. "I thought I heard the bell. What can I do for you?"

He had an open boyish face with freckles sprinkled across pale, clear skin. His light brown hair was cropped close to the side of his head and erupted in curls on top, giving his elfin ears a prominence they wouldn't have had with a different haircut. He wore a denim shirt with sleeves rolled up to the elbows, a narrow knitted tie of charcoal gray, and a double breasted vest of gray and brown glen plaid that looked like it had been part of a three piece suit about forty years ago.

I walked up to the desk. "I'm Louisa McGuire. I made an appointment—"

"Right, yes, I saw your name in the book. What kind of portrait are you looking for?"

"Actually, I don't need any pictures taken. I wanted to find out more about one of the pictures in your window display."

He cocked his head. "Okay. Um, those are all vintage photos from our files. Some of them are pretty old."

"Yes, it's a great display. Could I—would it be possible to see one of them more closely? The one in the corner of a young woman holding a baby?"

"Sure. No problem. Let me grab the key to the display area." He turned back to the door behind him. Opening it, he looked over his shoulder at me. "I'll be right back."

"I won't run away," I assured him.

San Francisco

Midcentury

60

Susan Rinaldi stood at the open door to the heavy-bodied airplane, greeting passengers as they came up the stairs and directing them to their seats. She peered at the straggling line of travelers approaching from the lighted terminal, and her attention was snagged by the couple with the baby. She smothered a sigh. Babies cried when the pressure in their ears became uncomfortable. They didn't know how to relieve it, and handing them a stick of chewing gum was not an option. And then everyone on board became irritated, especially on a long night flight like this one from San Francisco to New York.

She went on smiling and saying hello to each passenger as they entered. When the couple with the baby arrived in front of her she gave them a warm greeting as her practiced glance took in a number of details.

The man was tall and broad shouldered, probably in his early thirties, with sandy hair swept back from his forehead. His cashmere topcoat was black, unbuttoned over a dark gray suit, and the black wing-tip shoes were highly polished. He had grayish blue eyes under light brows, and his face was round and full lipped.

The woman was tiny. Her head barely topped the man's shoulder, a charming hat with a small veil perched on her dark hair. The crimson lips were drawn into a tense line, and Susan got an instant impression that this woman was holding in enormous anger. Her navy blue suit was double breasted, with red and white piping outlining the lapels and large red buttons with white centers marching down the front. One of the buttons was missing.

The man held the baby, and as soon as Susan saw the child's little face, she forgot her annoyance at the prospect of the crying that was to come. This child looked exhausted. Her blond curls were disheveled and her face streaked with tears. She was wearing a little dress with smocked Scotties across the front and matching rompers over her diaper, but the dress was crumpled, and Susan's nose told her there was a wet diaper that needed changing. The man held the baby awkwardly, facing out, and the woman kept her back to them.

"What an adorable baby," Susan said, giving the child her best crinkly-eyed smile. She reached out to tickle her tummy, and got a little smile in response that showed a couple of tiny bottom teeth. "If you need to change her, there should be room on the counter in the first class bathroom. Your seats are on the left, three rows back. "When everyone gets seated, I could warm a bottle for her. It will help settle her during take-off."

The woman marched off without speaking, but the man paused to give Susan a brief smile. "Thanks," he said. "My—my wife hasn't been well and this trip came up suddenly. The baby's, uh, nanny wasn't able to come with us and we're kind of out of our depth."

"Oh, you'll do just fine. She must be your daughter, she has your eyes." Susan noted again how tired the baby's blue-gray eyes looked, and when she glanced at the man his eyes looked nearly as weary.

He gave her another brief smile, nodded, and followed the dark haired woman back to their seats.

9

"Here we go," the photographer said cheerfully, holding up a key. "Which picture did you want to see?"

"The one in the corner nearest the door. Woman and baby."

"Oh, yeah, that one."

The display window was backed with frosted glass that opened like the back of a jewelry store display case. He inserted the key in the lock and slid the panel to the side, revealing the backs of the pictures within. Carefully picking up the photograph by the frame, he closed the glass and turned back to me.

"Have a seat." He gestured to the straight-backed chair in front of the desk. He placed the picture flat on the desk and went around to the other side, seating himself in the vintage leather office chair.

I settled on the seat he had indicated and set my purse and the canvas bag on the floor. Then I picked up the picture, holding the side edges of the frame between my hands, and stared at the two faces looking back at me. My own face was reflected in the glass over the photo, superimposed on the young woman's. I tilted it quickly to make the reflection disappear, trying to ignore the feeling of unease that constricted my throat. After a moment I had to look away. Just as the first time I saw the picture, I felt myself falling into the woman's face, not knowing if I were seeing myself or not. I blinked and looked again, concentrating on the child's dress.

Across the desk, the young man stirred. "You know, you look a lot like her."

I shook my head. "It's not me."

"Oh no, I know that. It couldn't be. This woman would be, let's see..." He figured in his head. "She would have been close to eighty now. And clearly you are nowhere near eighty." He gave me a cheeky grin.

"Maybe I am eighty and just very well preserved." I couldn't help grinning back.

"If you are, I want to know your secret. But in any case, there's no way you could be her. I'm afraid she died a long time ago."

"What? No." I suddenly realized how much I had hoped to meet this woman, whoever she was. I felt bereft, which must have shown.

He was instantly contrite.

"I'm so sorry, I didn't mean—"

"No, it's all right. I—I never knew her. I have no idea who she is. But you're right, I do look like her. In fact..."

I laid the photo back on the desk and reached down for the canvas bag. Taking out the envelope, I pulled out a five by seven print and handed it to him. He stared at the picture, then raised his eyes to me, then back at the picture.

"Wow," he said. "I'm getting goosebumps. This is you, right?"

I nodded. "Taken just after I got engaged, when I was twenty-five."

"The resemblance is uncanny." He reached for the framed photo and held the two side by side. "Looking at them together, I can spot a few differences. Your hairline is slightly higher on your forehead, eyebrows a little less slanted. Though hers might have been shaped cosmetically. Her lower lip is just a shade fuller than yours. Too bad the ears aren't showing in either picture. Ears are a dead giveaway."

"You have a good eye for detail."

"I was trained by the best," he said proudly. "I grew up in this studio. My great grandfather started it back in 1938."

"Was it...was it by any chance in Oakland back in the Fifties?"

"Yes! It was there until the early Sixties. They had to move because the state tore down whole neighborhoods to build the interstate highways. When my granddad took over, he found this spot in Berkeley and we've been here ever since. How did you know about Oakland?"

"I was born there. It was just a guess, really. I mean, it's on my birth certificate, but my parents never talked about their time in California."

"You must somehow be related to this woman."

"Maybe." I thought about the little dress in the bag next to me. "That's probably a simpler explanation than running into my doppelganger. I wonder, do you know anything else about this picture? How did it happen to get into your window?"

He nodded. "I know a little, but you need to talk to my granddad. He was here the other day helping me change out the pics on display. We change them every three or four weeks. There are hundreds of prints stored in the vault, and he gets a kick out of going through them. On his good days he can tell you the story of just about every portrait. I don't think he said much about this one. In fact, now that I think about it he got really quiet when he was framing it up."

"Darn, I was hoping he'd filled you in on her whole history."

"Why don't you go talk to him?"

"Really? Could I?"

"Of course. He'd love it. Of course he may talk your hind leg off. And he does have the occasional off day when he's a bit wandery."

"I would really love to pay him a visit," I said. "I'm not sure how long I'll be in town, but—I hope this doesn't sound too crazy, but it feels important to find out more."

"Not crazy at all. I mean, the resemblance is undeniable. I think it would be crazy not to follow up on it. Why don't you give me your contact info, and I'll give granddad a call later. I think he said he was meeting his cronies this afternoon. They hang out at Starbucks and drink hot chocolate." He pulled out a desk drawer and removed a piece of letterhead. "Here. And here's a pen."

I wrote down my name and cell number. "Do you have a card?" I asked.

"Sure." He pulled a card from his vest pocket and handed it to me. It was of thick, cream colored paper embossed on the front with the words

Studio 38

Portraits by Gallagher

On the back, contact information was printed in small red metallic type in the lower right hand corner.

"Classy card. So your name is Gallagher?"

"Nate Gallagher the third, at your service." He reached over the desk, and we shook hands.

Oakland, Mid Century

The air between them crackled with a surge of excitement as she handed him three checks.

"Tonight's the night, then." His smile had a look of satisfaction that she knew well. It gave her the same sense of power that it did in bed. "I'll deposit these in the three banks, and this time tomorrow we'll be in New York." He looked at the top check and shook his head. "Baby, you sign his name even better than he does."

"Thank you, kind sir." Joan rose from the chair in front of her boss's large desk and picked up the check ledger. "Frank certainly picked the right moment to go to Palm Springs."

"I think he's got a woman down there. That's where he always runs off to celebrate, and when the funds arrived yesterday from the Bank of America he couldn't be out of here fast enough. All right, let me get these deposited."

"Don't forget to call your wife first." As always, the word "wife" had a razor sharp edge.

He laughed. "As if I would. Relax. You know she'll do whatever I tell her. Everything is under control."

He walked down the short hallway to his own office, where he picked up the heavy black receiver of the telephone on his desk. "Florrie, put me through to my wife, would you? Thanks, hon."

A couple of miles away, the ringing phone startled Eloise. "Hello?"

"Hi, baby, it's me."

"Carter! Hi. What a surprise. I mean—"

"Can't a guy call his cute little wife in the afternoon to invite her out for a celebration dinner?"

"Really? Oh, that's—what are we celebrating?"

"That big deal we've been working on came through."

"How wonderful! This was that bank thing? I'm so proud of you."

"Well, thanks, hon. I think your dad is going to be proud too, and there should be a nice bonus in it for yours truly. So you girls put on your best dresses and meet me at Luigi's at eight, okay?"

"Okay. Did you say girls, plural?"

"Sure. Bring the baby, why not. I'm sure Luigi can rustle up a high chair."

"Oh, but—maybe my sister could babysit. I'll call her now—"

His tone changed in an instant. "I said bring the baby. Eloise. Could you just once do what you're told? Jesus."

Eloise bit her lip, trying to keep the tears at bay. "I'm sorry, darling. Of course I'll bring her."

He switched back to his affable self. "That's better. I've got to go, errands to run. I'll see you at Luigi's. And Eloise..."

"Yes, Carter?"

"Don't worry if I'm a little late. I've got some work to catch up on while your dad is away and I'm not sure just how long it will take. Order us a carafe of wine, and I'll get away from the office as quick as I can tonight." As he hung up the phone, he thought, at least that bit is true. The last place anyone would want to be tonight is this office.

10

Bob rang the bell. Immediately the door was flung open.

"Bob! Welcome!" A man about my age stood back and motioned us inside the house with a flourish of his hand. His gray hair swept back from a high forehead, and the small mustache and Van Dyke beard were impeccably groomed. "Did you find a place to park? And this—" he took my right hand between both of his and gazed deeply into my eyes— "this must be Louisa. My dear, I have heard so much about you. Welcome."

"Thank you. What a lovely home." I unstuck my eyes from his and glanced around.

"We just love it," he said in a confiding tone. "I'll give you a tour in a bit, shall I?"

"I'll look forward to it."

"Louisa, this is Erik Landisen. Eric was part of the team that went to Central America last summer."

Erik beamed at me, still holding my hand between his two warm and ever so slightly damp palms. I wasn't sure how to extricate it politely, but after a couple more seconds ticked by I thought impatiently, for heaven's sake, you can't stand here all night. Reclaim your hand. I turned my wrist a bit and pulled, and he let go. I waited until he turned to Bob to slide my hand into my pocket to wipe my palm.

"But come in, come in! Several people are here already. You'll find drinks on the sideboard, and Maria seems to have stashed food all over the place."

"Ah, a treasure hunt," I commented.

Erik laughed immoderately.

"Bob, she's priceless! Treasure hunt indeed."

Bob caught my eye, and I had to look away to keep from laughing. Fortunately the doorbell rang just then, and Erik turned away to answer it. Bob steered me into the large living room, where three women and a young man stood talking by the raised hearth of a large free-standing fireplace, its magnificent copper hood rising to the high beamed ceiling. At our appearance their conversation ceased so quickly that I wondered if we had been the topic under discussion.

"Bob! Hi!" One of the women broke away to approach us. "You made it. Did you find a place to park? This must be Louisa."

Bob nodded. "Louisa, this is Maria Delgado."

Maria shook my hand enthusiastically as I smiled at her. "Louisa, I am very happy to meet you at last. I have heard so much about you from Bob I feel I know you already."

I murmured something in reply, feeling distinctly at a disadvantage, for I had heard nothing of her. I assumed she was the Maria who had scattered food around for us to find. She was wearing a sleeveless hot-pink silk top over flowing Palazzo pants in a bright paisley. I wondered if she had dressed to match the period of the house.

Bob touched my arm. "What would you like to drink?"

"Oh, um, anything. Wine. Whatever."

"Red or white?"

"I guess red. But only if it's open."

"Oh yes, plenty of reds to choose from," Maria put in. "Bob, bring her a glass of the Nebbiolo. It's quite special."

"Will do," he said cheerfully, and left me with Maria.

"You will love this wine," she purred. "We brought it back on our last trip to Italy."

"How wonderful."

Another of the women from the group by the fireplace approached. "Hi," she smiled at me. "I'm Debbie. You must be Louisa."

I smiled back as we shook hands. She was younger than Maria, perhaps early thirties. Her straight hair was dyed Smurf blue and grazed her shoulders, with bangs that ended an inch above her brows, which were also blue. "Nice to meet you."

"I've heard so much about you from Bob," Debbie added.

"Ah. Well."

So here's the thing: I absolutely loathe being told that someone has heard so much about me. Any speck of paranoia I've ever experienced comes back in full force.

You say you've heard about me, so what exactly is it you know?

And there's no good reply. Do you say "thank you," or "oh, really?" Or, "oh yes and I've heard about you" (which you haven't so you're hoping desperately that they don't call you on it).

I kept a broad smile on my face and managed not to demand to know exactly what Bob had been saying about me.

Debbie turned to Maria. "I'd have known she was Bob's Louisa anywhere, wouldn't you?"

Maria nodded enthusiastically. "Oh yes. I think if I'd seen her walking down the street, I would have said that must be Louisa."

A scene began to play on the movie screen behind my eyes. Cheering spectators lined the street as I followed a marching band playing something by Sousa. Twirlers flung batons high in the air, and two hunky young men carried a banner over my head that read "It's Louisa!" in sparkling gold foot-high letters.

"What a wonderful house," I interjected, banishing my personal parade. "Was it built, when? Fifties? Sixties? I always love the openness of post and beam construction."

"Why yes," Maria answered. "Late Fifties. Erik can tell you everything about the architect but I confess all that just leaks out of my brain. Are you an architect? Bob never said."

"Oh no, I just like houses. I help my cousin in her antique store, and midcentury pieces are quite sought after these days."

"Oh really, an antique store. How interesting."

Maria could not have sounded less interested if she had tried for a week. But I felt myself relax a little. If Bob had really talked about me, he would have mentioned that I work in my cousin's store. I felt a little safer.

Fortunately Bob returned just then and handed me a large tulip-shaped pinot noir glass half filled with a dark liquid.

"Here you go," he said. "I made sure to get the Nebbiolo. Debbie, good to see you."

She beamed at him. "Hi, Bob." There was noticeable warmth in her voice.

"How did your sessions go this afternoon?" Looking at me, he added, "Debbie's using clinical hypnosis as the basis for her dissertation. She's part of the same research project at the university that I am."

"Oh, I wish you'd been there. You would really have appreciated the nuances I got from one of the subjects."

I sipped my wine.

The inside of my mouth shriveled.

What the hell was this stuff? I've had a fair amount of wine over the years and I appreciate a dry red far more than anything on the sweet end of the continuum, but this was beyond dry. This was the Sahara distilled into a glass. I hastily swallowed.

"Isn't that delicious?" Maria watched me closely.

"Mmmmm." I nodded. "This is—in a class of its own."

Her smile was smug. "See, I knew that was the right wine for you, from everything Bob has told us."

I couldn't look at him. What could he possibly have said that had led to my being presented with this swill?

"Thank you," I told Maria. "This is really special. Um, could you direct me to the bathroom?"

"Of course. This way."

Bob reached out a hand. "I can hold your glass for you," he offered.

"That's okay, I'll just sip along the way."

No way was I going to hand over this glass of liquid alum. It was going down the drain the instant I locked that bathroom door behind me. Probably would do the drain a lot of good.

Another short film began to play in my head, in which a plumber told Maria and Erik that all their drains were in terrible condition, except for the one in the downstairs bathroom which for some reason was completely clear. Though showing signs of corrosion not seen in any of the others.

Maria led me through the kitchen and down a short hall into a laundry room. "Here you go." She pointed to a door that was slightly ajar, just past the dryer. I thanked her and she swished away, the voluminous pants flowing around her like the hair on a well-groomed Afghan hound.

I went into the bathroom, which proved to be claustrophobically small, and pulled the door closed behind me. The opposite wall was about three feet from my nose. On my left, a pink toilet. On my right, a pink basin affixed to the wall under a framed mirror.

I poured the wine into the sink, hoping it wouldn't leave any evidence on the vintage porcelain. I should have known it would splash and leave a stain on the tunic I'd worn for the occasion. Three small red spots bloomed at waist level, turning dark purple on the cobalt blue fabric. I stared down at myself.

Immediately an internal debate raged. You should rinse that out right now! What, and go back out among those people with a huge wet spot on your top instead of these little tiny stains? No way.

If I had a hair dryer, I could dry the fabric. Of course it would be noisy and take a long time. But who would hear me, back in the maid's territory behind the laundry room? I glanced around. Of course there was no dryer.

Looking straight into the mirror I muttered, "It's nothing. No one will even notice. At least I don't have to drink any more of that wine."

I carefully set my glass on the edge of the sink, next to a plastic container of liquid soap. I turned on the cold tap to rinse away any evidence of my deceit, rinsed my hands for good measure, turned off the tap and looked for a towel. There was none. No hand towel, no paper towels. Only the toilet paper in its little roller niche. I shook my hands and wiped my fingers on my pants. Picking up the glass, I left.

I could tell by the noise level beyond the kitchen that more people had arrived. The voices were loud and convivial. Immediately I was transported to the parties my husband Roger used to insist that I attend. Large gatherings of his colleagues and clients with too much booze and too much noise and never a single person who was interested in speaking to me.

I wanted to run away.

Trays of finger foods lined the kitchen counters. I paused to inspect one holding tiny quiches decorated with snips of chives. I popped one in my mouth just as a man arrived at the kitchen door. He was mid-fiftyish, wearing a Harris tweed sport coat over a charcoal gray turtleneck that matched his gray loafers.

"Hey, hon," he called, barely glancing at me, "Maria says you need to bring out a couple more trays of food."

He left. I stared after him. Seriously? Did he think I was the caterer? Or had Maria told him to go ask Bob's girlfriend to bring out more food? Perhaps she would expect me to scatter the trays about as she had done. And do the dishes later.

I grabbed another little quiche (they were tasty) and moved through the kitchen. "At least he didn't say he'd heard a lot about me," I growled to myself. In the dining room beyond I hastened to the sideboard and quickly scanned the bottles of wine there. Ah. A pinot noir from southern Oregon. I poured an inch into my glass, hoping the color was close enough to pass as Nebbiolo. Swirling my glass, I strolled on, back to the living room, where I scanned the crowd of thirty or more people for Bob. He's tall enough that he's usually easy to find.

But he was nowhere in sight.

Oakland, Mid Century

Eloise smoothed foundation on her face, then squeezed a tiny bit of rouge out of a little tube and rubbed it on her cheekbone. She peeked in the mirror at little Louisa, who was sitting on the floor near the bed. The baby held a nubby ball and was inspecting it carefully with her mouth.

"Ick, Louisa, don't eat that."

Louisa removed the toy from her mouth and gave her mother a drooly smile. Eloise smiled back.

"Can you believe your daddy invited us both to dinner? That's got to be a good thing. Don't you think so? So we're going to look pretty and you are going to be a very, very good girl."

Louisa gurgled. Eloise returned to her makeup. A dusting of powder, a little eye shadow. She leaned forward to inspect her arched brows.

"I swear, where do these hairs come from? I mean, overnight. You close your eyes and when you open them, it's time to pluck your brows."

"Bah bah bah," the baby said solemnly.

"Exactly." Eloise reached for the tweezers, glancing at the baby in the mirror again. Louisa was rocking on her diapered bottom, and managed to roll herself forward onto hands and knees.

"Look at you, starting to crawl. I bet you're going to be a speed demon, aren't you?" Eloise plucked the errant hairs, wincing a little at the pain. "Ouch. Okay, let me get my dress on and then we'll get you ready. Hmmm, if you're going to be crawling, your daddy had better put up that baby gate at the top of the stairs. Or maybe Lennie and I could do it. We don't want you getting hurt."

She rose from the dressing table and turned to her closet. Louisa scooted along the floor. Her mother stepped over and picked her up, holding her in front of her face. "Hey, Miss Smarty Pants, you can crawl! Are you just the smartest, cutest baby ever?"

She kissed the baby's nose and set her back down. "All right, stay in Mommy's room and don't fall down the stairs."

Eloise went to her walk-in closet, which still seemed like an unnecessary luxury. Now that the war had been over for more than ten years, clothing was in plentiful supply, but she still didn't see how any one person could fill a closet this size. Although Carter had done a pretty good job. And she had to admit that the petticoat for her taffeta dress took up plenty of space on its own.

She took off her satin robe, tossing it onto the bed, then pulled the petticoat off its hanger and over her head. Before putting on the dress, she inspected it to make sure there were no spots from its wearing to the photography studio. She breathed out a little sigh of relief; still clean. Carter hated spots, hated mess of any kind. And try as she might, spots and mess just went hand in hand with taking care of a baby.

"Louisa?" she called. "Are you being a good girl?"

She slid the dress on, then struggled to zip it. The little tab finally reached the top, but the hook and eye closure didn't want to catch. "I'll be glad when you're big enough to do zippers and hooks. Of course, maybe by then daddy will be around more and he can do me up."

She picked up the shoes that went with the dress and carried them out of the closet. "Might as well wait to put these on until you're dressed. Oh, wait, I'd better put a robe over this dress until we're ready to go."

She dropped the shoes and turned back to the closet, then stopped. "Louisa? Where are you, baby?"

A cold surge of panic swept over her. No baby in sight. She hurried to the bedroom door and out into the hall, but Louisa was not to be seen. She ran to the stairway and looked down, but was spared the dreaded sight of a baby at the bottom.

She turned back to the bedroom. "Louisa? Where are you?"

A faint "Bah bah bah!" answered her. She followed the sound to her husband's closet. The door was open about a foot. She pulled it wider and flipped up the light switch by the door.

"Mah! Mamama!" Louisa blinked in the light and gave her a huge smile.

"Louisa! What are you doing in here? You know daddy would have a fit if he saw you." Eloise tried to make her voice stern, but she couldn't help smiling back at the child. Louisa was surrounded by Carter's shoes and was holding a slipper that Eloise had knitted. The baby banged the slipper on the floor, then put the toe in her mouth.

"That can't taste good. Though I'm sure it's perfectly clean because your daddy never put it on even once. If you had some top teeth as well as those cute little bottom teeth I bet you could chew a hole in that thing, and daddy would never notice in a million years."

She reached down to take the slipper away, but Louisa gripped it tighter and twisted away. The movement made her lose her balance and she rolled onto her back. Eloise watched the expressions on her baby's face—surprise, then chagrin, then acceptance—and the slipper went back into the mouth.

"Shoot, just go ahead and enjoy that old slipper. For sure you're the only one who ever will. You just wait there for a minute while I go slip my robe over this dress so you can't drool on me. Yes you do, my sweetie, you are a drooly girl. And I'm sure you will try to eat my buttons if I don't cover them up." She stepped closer to the baby and tickled her tummy, getting a gurgle in response. "You are an old drooly button eater girl, that's what you are."

Eloise straightened and looked around the closet. Her eyes narrowed. Something seemed...wrong. She looked along the line of work shirts, then casual shirts, then sport coats...that was it. There weren't as many pieces as the last time she had been in here. The hangars were still evenly spaced, but here and there was an empty one. She looked at the bar that held his slacks; several empty hangers there too. Had he decided he had too many clothes and cleared out some of the oldest?

But no, there was that old denim shirt with the hole in the pocket, and the pants with the patched knee that he wore to mow the grass. She looked down at Louisa amid the shoes, and tried to remember which pair he had put on that morning. The black wing tips, because he'd worn his charcoal suit. But the brown loafers seemed to be missing from the closet, and the golf shoes, and those new short brown boots with the zipper up the sides that she thought made him look like a beatnik.

"Louisa, did you eat daddy's shoes?"

The baby looked at her, blue-gray eyes wide, then she babbled, "Bah mah mah pah."

"Okay, I believe you," her mother replied. Then she noticed Carter's terry bathrobe draped over something at the end of the closet. "Did you pull daddy's bathrobe down? Though I don't see how you could, you're not standing yet."

Eloise picked up the bathrobe and hung it on its usual hook by the door, then noticed the shining brown leather suitcase it had been draped over.

She suddenly found it difficult to breathe. Her heart thumped once, twice, three times as she stared at the case, then she gasped in some air. Without conscious thought, she grabbed the handle of the case and pulled. It was quite heavy. She dragged it out of the closet and managed to heave it onto the bed. She pushed the latches. They were locked.

"Damn." The word slipped out, and she looked toward the closet guiltily, hoping Louisa hadn't heard. She glared down at the case, then thought of something. Her own suitcase was the same brand as his, purchased for their honeymoon trip. Maybe the key would work. But where had she put it? She hurried to her dressing table and pulled out drawers, rummaging within, but no little key. Her gaze fell on her ring box and she grabbed it up. Pulling open the lid, she dumped the contents out and scrabbled through. There, the key. She picked it up and carried it to the case on the bed.

Snap! First one lock, then the other sprang open. Taking a deep breath, she lifted the lid of the case.

It was full. Shirts, pants, socks, shoes. His shaving kit. A manicure kit. Two extra belts. A sport coat.

Suddenly her knees were trembling and wouldn't hold her. She sank onto the floor next to the bed, her taffeta dress billowing about her.

"He must be going on a business trip and forgot to tell me," she said aloud.

From the closet came an answering gurgle from Louisa. In a moment the baby came crawling through the closet door and scooted to her mother, delighted to see her sitting on the floor. Eloise gathered the baby into her lap and leaned over her protectively. It was then she realized that tears were streaming down her face. Louisa reached out a little starfish hand and patted her cheek.

"Oh, honey, oh Louisa, do you think—is your daddy—do you think he's leaving us?"

Louisa gave her mother a serious look. "Mah," she said.

"He is, isn't he? He's all packed and ready to go and he's just going to walk out that door."

Eloise realized that her emotions were a jumble, she hardly knew what she felt. Fear. What would they do? How would they live? Well, surely her father wouldn't let them starve. Of course he would blame her. She could already hear his scathing voice berating her for not being the kind of wife a man like Carter needed. And that was the moment when she knew that overriding her fear was anger. And realizing that she was angry let loose the floodgates she had kept so carefully locked.

She began to shake. How dare he. How dare he treat her like this. Like...like a tiresome plaything. Something worth only his contempt. No matter how hard she had tried to please him, she had reaped only coldness. She *had* tried, she had done everything she could think of, she had stuffed her real personality down so deep inside her that she now thought of her true self as a little hard, dark nub hiding in a deep silent cave. And for what?

To be left sitting with her darling baby in an Italian restaurant, toying with bread sticks and sipping from a carafe of red wine while he disappeared with his carefully packed suitcase into the night.

Louisa gave a little cry, and she realized she was gripping her child so tightly that there might be bruises.

"Oh sweetie, I'm so sorry. It's not you, I'm not mad at you. Never at you, darling. You are the only good thing in my life."

She leaned over and kissed the golden curls on top of Louisa's head. Then she rose with the child in her arms, knowing where she was going.

"Come on, Louisa. Let's put on your dress, your picture dress, and then we'll go downstairs and put your bottle in the diaper bag. And then we are going to pay daddy a visit."

Louisa gave one of her gurgles, then blew spit bubbles at her mother. Eloise hiccupped a laugh.

"That's right. We are going to pay daddy a surprise visit and tell him a thing or two. And if you want to get spit bubbles on him, please do."

11

I nudged my way between groups of party goers, peering this way and that, looking for Bob. Could he have wandered outside? Maybe he had gone off with that Debbie, she looked like she really liked him. I didn't really think he was capable of such a thing, but on the other hand it would immediately solve my dilemma over whether to stay or return to Willow Falls.

I kept a smile on my face, which must have looked more genuine than it felt, for I received a couple of brief answering smiles. But no one spoke as I passed, and no group parted to include me. I saw a comfortable-looking pair of empty chairs in a corner and made my way past the fireplace, around a large red leather sofa, and settled into one of them. The wall of glass beside me gave a magnificent view of twinkling city lights, with San Francisco Bay a channel of darkness in the distance.

Abandoning my smile for the moment, I took a sip of the pinot I'd poured in the kitchen. Damn. This wine was seriously good, rich and mellow, hints of raspberries in the finish. I wished I had poured a larger tot into my glass.

With another sip, I tore my gaze away from the view and surveyed the party crowd. Mostly middle age, middle class, the occasional student to liven the mix. Scraps of conversation rose above the hum of noise—he never said any...Belinda, you didn't!...but the way the scans revealed altered activity in the fusiform regions involved...for three hundred thousand in the Eighties and now they want five million... I was content to let it flow by. None of it had anything to do with me.

If I stayed here with Bob, these would likely be our friends. Immediately came the answering thought, like hell they will.

Movement by my feet caught my attention. A small red Abyssinian cat poked a head out from beneath the other chair. The peach-colored nose sniffed my foot.

"Mewp," said the cat, and slid out from under the chair. She jumped into my lap.

"Good evening, Miss Kitty. You are a miss? It's very nice to meet you." I ran a hand down her sleek russet back, adding a little scratch at the base of the tail.

She turned on her motor, circled once, then settled on my lap with paws tucked in. Together we watched the party. I noticed a small plate on the table at my elbow that held a selection of canapes

"I'm a little peckish," I confided to the cat. "How about you? Do you suppose this is someone's plate, or is it part of the treasure hunt for food?"

"Prrrt."

"Yes, that's what I thought too. Let's try this one." I picked up a tiny tart, breaking off a crumb of the white cheese before popping the pastry into my mouth. I chewed, and offered the cheese to the cat, who sniffed it and then licked it off my finger. "Goat cheese, I think. The red stuff must have been roasted beet. Shall we try another?"

I took another sip of wine and noticed a group of women chatting nearby. They were close to the wall of glass, but none seemed to notice the amazing view. Whatever their topic of conversation, it was providing them with plenty of mirth. As they laughed, the two with their backs to me shifted position, and I saw that they were talking to Maria and Debbie. I put the smile back on my face just in case they might glance my way and returned my attention to the food.

"Which one appeals to you, Miss Kitty?" She raised her nose and sniffed, then blinked her amber eyes at me. "Oooh, no, maybe not that one, I don't like cucumber. How about this tofu lollipop thing? Oh, you don't like tofu. Okay, we'll compromise with this, is this hummus? You'll like it, it's from your part of the world."

She did like the hummus, licking a dollop enthusiastically from my finger as I ate the rest.

When it was gone, she cleaned up my finger, then finished by making sure her whiskers were tidy.

"You look fine," I assured her. "Perfect. No spots on you, are there?"

"Mmurrp."

"Thanks. I appreciate that."

The volume from the group of women suddenly rose, and the cat and I looked their way.

"Oh good, Adler Beck is here. Adler!" Debbie waved to someone in the direction of the door. Above the crowd I saw a graceful return wave. In a moment another woman approached.

She was gorgeous. Tawny skin that was probably a result of any number of ethnic groups mixing in this California melting pot, dark auburn hair swept up into a real live French twist, a 'do I hadn't see on anyone under the age of eighty in years. The dress had either come from a very expensive vintage clothing shop or perhaps from a very expensive grandmother's closet; if I had to guess, the label in that pink wool jacket probably said Pierre Cardin. Perhaps Lanvin. I tried to memorize the details so I could share them with Kay later.

It was fascinating to watch the ritual of air kisses from this angle, below and behind.

"Darlings!" Her voice was perfectly modulated to rise just above the din. "So wonderful to see you all. Maria, everything looks lovely. What perfectly beautiful food."

"Thank you kindly, ma'am." Maria dropped a sketch of a curtsy. "I admit I'm very good at hiring caterers."

"The best." Debbie nodded, beaming at the newcomer. Her admiration for—was it Adler? Adelle? whatever—made me think of a Golden Retriever puppy. If she'd had a tail, it would have been sweeping all the knickknacks from the coffee table behind her.

"I saw Bob talking to Erik and Pablo in the alcove," the woman said. Oh good, I thought, I'll go find him in a bit. She went on, "So did that woman show up? Or is she still driving around the fly-over lands with a pack of dogs?"

"She's here someplace, or she was," Maria answered. She added another sentence, but I couldn't hear what it was. Whatever she said, it made the other women laugh.

I felt my eyebrow lift, and I settled back in my comfortable chair. The cat rose and stretched, then turned and butted her head against my chin. She climbed up my front and settled around the back of my neck with her paws draped over my shoulder.

"Momow," she chirped in my ear.

I reached up to scratch her neck. "You said it, baby. You could not be more right."

The cat and I murmured remarks about other party goers for perhaps ten or fifteen minutes. Then there was a stirring among the chatting groups, and I caught sight of Bob coming my way. He saw me in my corner and waved, his face alight.

The movement of his wave alerted Debbie to his approach. "Bob, look who's here! It's Adler."

Bob paused by their group. "Hi Adler, long time. Bonnie. Theresa." He nodded to the other two women.

"Much too long," Adler drawled. One corner of her mouth turned up. She moved closer to him so that she could look up into his face. "And what are you doing here alone? I thought your, um, friend would have arrived by now."

He nodded. "She did. She has. She's right over there." He sent one of his best smiles in my direction.

The cat and I smiled back.

12

"I'm awfully sorry about deserting you last night," Bob said. "Erik started talking shop and I couldn't get away from him."

We were strolling down the hill to have breakfast at one of the local eateries. We'd left the dogs happily gnawing on chew toys in the back yard so we wouldn't be limited to the places with dog-friendly patios.

"Not a problem. It was interesting seeing you among colleagues. I think it's the first time I've had that experience."

"I'm not sure a party shows any of us in our true collegial light. I hope you got to talk to at least a few interesting people."

"I thoroughly enjoyed the cat."

"She did make a wonderful accessory around your neck like that."

"Actually, I completely fell in love with her. You wouldn't like to sound them out to see if they would part with her, would you?"

"Hmmm. Not sure how I would go about that. But I'll watch for an opening. I thought Adler seemed quite taken with you."

You must be joking, I thought in astonishment. Aloud, I contented myself with an innocuous, "She seems like an interesting person."

Bob is a very nice guy, but no more sensitive to social nuance than most men. His pleasure at seeing me the previous evening in the chair with my Abyssinian neckpiece had been obvious. He had left the group of women and hurried to me. I stood, cat balancing easily, and took his hand. Over his shoulder I had seen Adler's face, and how her eyes narrowed slightly as she looked at us.

Bob had led me back to the group and made introductions. "Nice to meet you all," I'd said, looking at the two who had had their backs to me. To Maria I had added, "Your cat and I have had the most interesting conversation."

"Grizelda, you bad cat, you know I was looking for you." She flashed a brief smile. "So kind of you to put up with her. I tried to find her earlier to shut her away downstairs. I know a couple of our guests are allergic. May I?" She reached up to take the cat, who hooked her claws into my shirt in protest. "Grizelda, let go."

I had murmured into her pointed ear, "Sorry, sweetheart. We'll meet again." I plucked her off my shoulder and handed her over to Maria, who carried her away, telling her again what a bad cat she was. Before a new topic of conversation might start, I had turned to Bob. "We should probably think about heading home in a bit. After all, I have that pack of dogs to take care of."

He had laughed. "Yes, quite a pack, all right. I'm ready if you are."

Debbie flicked a quick look at Adler, whose expression remained aloof. The younger woman's cheeks turned pink, and she dropped her eyes to the floor.

"Perhaps I'll see you again while I'm here," I'd said to the group. "Debbie, lovely to meet you, good luck with your research project. Good night, Adele."

Before she could correct me, I'd led Bob away. I don't think he noticed I'd gotten the name wrong. My inner bitch, who delights in passive aggressive behavior, had cackled gleefully.

I'm only human.

Down in the little shopping district, we decided to try the Salvadoran place for breakfast. Bob ordered *huevos revueltos,* which proved to be eggs scrambled with onions, tomato, peppers and cheese. My *desayuno salvadoreno* included eggs, plantains, and a pupusa. We were just tackling our plates when I heard someone say my name. I looked around, and recognized Nate Gallagher the Third from the photography studio following the waiter to a table.

"Nate, hi. How are you?"

He paused by my chair. "I'm good. I see you've found my favorite breakfast place."

"Mmm, I love it. Can you join us? Oh, this is my friend Bob Richardson. Bob, Nate runs the photography studio up the street."

The two men shook hands, and Bob gestured to the spare chair at our table. "Join us."

So Nate sat down. The waiter realized Nate had stopped following him, and returned to our table. "Ah, you find friends, very good. The usual?"

"Please, Alberto. Thanks."

I had a sudden stab of homesickness. How many times had I heard Cleta at the Bluebird Café say, "The usual?" in exactly the same way?

"I was going to call you this morning," Nate said, looking at me. "I talked to my granddad and he said he'd love to meet you."

"Great." I turned to Bob. "Nate's grandfather was working at the photography studio when that picture we saw in the window was taken."

He looked enthusiastic. "That's wonderful. I bet you'll get all your questions answered."

Alberto returned with a steaming mug of coffee that he set in front of Nate. "Food soon," he promised, and headed off to seat a young couple with a baby in a pack peering over her father's shoulder.

"Did you set up a time with your grandfather, or should I call him?" I asked as Nate took a sip. He swallowed.

"Are you free this afternoon by any chance?"

I looked at Bob. "I think so. Do we have any plans for later?"

He made a face. "Damn. I've got to go into the office. I've got a new client who could only schedule for this afternoon."

"Oh. Well, that's okay. I'm sure I can find the house."

"I was hoping I could go with you."

"Me too, but I can tell you about it later."

I could wait until he's free, I told myself. But I didn't want to wait. I looked back at Nate. "This afternoon would be great. When and where?"

"He hopes you can come to his house. He doesn't drive much anymore. He says the less Bay Area traffic he has to drive in, the longer he's going to live. One way or another."

"I know just how he feels. Rush hour at home in Willow Falls is two cars backed up at a stop sign."

"After my car ended up at the bottom of a pond," Bob added, "I decided I could live perfectly well without one here. Makes me feel very cosmopolitan, actually."

Alberto arrived with a steaming plate of food that matched mine and slid it onto the table in front of Nate. "Here you go. Anyone need anything? Coffee?"

"May I have more hot water for my tea?" I asked.

"Of course. I will be right back."

Nate shoveled in some eggs with the enthusiasm of the young and fit. After he'd swallowed, he squinted at Bob. "You drove your car into a pond?"

I put my elbows on the table and covered my face with my hands. "No, I did. Sort of." I took my hands down and shrugged. "A friend was driving, and we—we were forced off the road. Scary, actually."

Bob's brow furrowed and he reached for my hand. "I'm sorry, Louisa, I shouldn't have brought it up."

"No, it's nothing. I—I guess I still feel a little guilty that your car is at the bottom of Quarry Pond." Guilty, yes, but even more I still had disquieting dreams of being in that car at the bottom of the pond, not knowing how we would be able to escape. I gave his hand a squeeze, then let it go and picked up my fork.

"Well, you can stop that. Now that you've experienced driving here, it should be obvious I'm better off without my car."

"Hey, I know what you should do," Nate put in. "In a few years when people have forgotten what happened, you could start a rumor about the haunted pond and the mysterious car down there."

Bob and I both laughed. "Great idea," he said, but I shook my head.

"Nate, in a small town nothing is ever forgotten. I bet in a hundred years they'll still be talking about how Louisa McGuire put that Honda in the pond."

"Wait till you meet my granddad," he countered. "I don't think he's ever forgotten anything either."

Oakland, Mid-Century

"Wait here, I'll just be a few minutes."

The cab driver nodded and turned on the radio. Carter jumped out of the cab and dashed up the steps

98

to the house. He used his key to open the front door and stepped inside.

All was quiet. Good. Eloise would be on her way to the restaurant. He had to hand it to Joan; her planning and attention to detail were first rate.

He took the stairs two at a time and hurried into the bedroom. He looked around, saying to himself as he had all day, "The last time. I'll never step foot in here again." The words charged him with a fizz of excitement. Even his name would change. His last day of being Carter Chessman; tomorrow he would be Randy Chelton again.

He spared a moment to remember the real Carter Chessman, who had quickly acquired the nickname of Pawn during basic training. No one had commented on the similarity of their names—Randall Charles Chelton and Robert Carter Chessman—but he'd been struck by it. And when Pawn died in Korea, he had quietly helped himself to the guy's identity papers, which seemed to have gone unnoticed. He'd had no end in view at the time; it just seemed like a good idea.

The air in the bedroom smelled of Eloise's perfume. Her blue silk robe was thrown onto the bed, and her makeup strewn across the dressing table instead of neatly stowed away as he preferred. He shrugged; after this she could be as messy as she liked. Joan was as neat and precise as a cat; it was one of the many things he loved about her. He smiled, remembering an unusual cat he had seen at someone's house. An Abyssinian, that was what they had called it. Maybe he would buy her one of those after they decided where they would live.

He walked to the dresser and pulled the third drawer out of the case. Overturning it on the bed, he removed the tape holding a long white envelope on the bottom. He slid the envelope into his jacket pocket. He thought about leaving the drawer there, but putting things away had been dinned into him as a child, and further ingrained in the Army. He returned the drawer to the case, gathered the socks and ties that had tumbled onto the bed and threw them back in. The tape he rolled into a tangled wad, throwing that into the drawer as well before closing it. He grinned suddenly, remembering the times as a boy he had gathered up all the scattered toys and clothes in his bedroom and stuffed them into a drawer, just before his father came in to check that he had cleaned up his room as he'd been ordered.

He felt young again, and free.

He turned to the closet, and his foot bumped something on the floor by the bed. Louisa's little teddy bear. She must have been playing in here while her mother got ready for the dinner date that wasn't going to happen.

Bending down, he picked up the toy and looked into its shiny shoe button eyes. He wouldn't miss Eloise; she was a good kid, but she would never measure up to Joan. Yet he had to admit, though it would take torture to make him say it to anyone else, he would kind of miss the baby. She was noisy and sometimes smelly, and she looked way too much like her mother, but the first time he had held her and seen his own eyes looking back at him, a piece of his heart had twisted inside his chest.

He made a motion to toss the little bear onto the bed, but found himself stuffing it into his jacket pocket instead. The envelope crackled.

"Get a grip," he muttered aloud. But he left the bear in his pocket.

13

I parked my car in a shady spot in front of the little California bungalow and rolled the windows down a few inches. From the passenger seat I picked up my purse and the bag holding the photos and the baby dress. "Okay, you guys be good," I said, looking over my shoulder at Emily Ann and Jack. "Take a nap. I'm not sure how long I will be, but after this we'll finally go find that dog park."

Jack thumped his strong tail enthusiastically at the word "park." When I opened the car door and got out, he jumped into the driver's seat.

"I'm taking the keys," I told him, holding up the ring and giving it a little shake. "Emily Ann, don't let him hot wire the car while I'm gone."

I straightened and looked at Nate's grandfather's house. A classic small Craftsman house with a broad front porch, deep eaves supported by wooden triangle braces, and a central front door between sets of triple windows on each side. Deep wooden window boxes overflowed with brightly colored flowers. To the right of the house, the driveway that led to a detached garage in back consisted of two narrow strips of paving. I could almost see a Model T sitting there.

I went through the white picket gate and started up the brick walk to the wide steps. The front door opened and an old man with flyaway white hair stepped out.

"Are those dogs in your car?" he called. "Bring them in."

I stopped halfway up the walk. "Are you sure? They'll be okay in the shade—"

"Bring 'em in, I love dogs."

I didn't need to be asked again. Returning to the car, I raised the back hatch and attached leashes to collars before letting the pair out. Emily Ann raised her long nose and tested the air, then followed Jack and me to the house. Jack hurried up the steps, his tail wagging his hind end as he approached the old man.

Nate's grandfather reached down a hand for both dogs to sniff. "Well, aren't you a pair," he crooned to them. In a nanosecond both crowded close to him, getting pats and scratches in just the right places. I had a chance to study him, and the resemblance to his grandson was strong. Same compact size and elfin ears. Like the younger Nate he wore a vest over a shirt with rolled up sleeves, though his vest was knitted, probably of cashmere. I wondered if the Nate of the generation between them looked like the third pea in the pod.

"Yes, you are, you are excellent fellows. Come on in, I've got dog cookies in the kitchen." He gave each dog a final pat and straightened, finally looking fully at me. His jaw dropped, and he swallowed. "El— Ellie?" he croaked. He gave his head a sharp shake. "No, you can't be. But—"

I stepped forward. "I'm Louisa McGuire," I said, holding out my hand. He took it between both of his, continuing to stare at my face. After a few seconds I began to wonder how to proceed. "Um, your grandson—"

"Forgive my manners," he said, releasing my hand. "It's just that the resemblance is so strong. You look just the way someone I knew long ago would look at your age." He stepped back into the house. "Come on in."

The door opened straight into the living room. To my left, an open door showed a comfortable den with a desk and a couple of overstuffed chairs. The living room was flooded with light from the triple front windows and two smaller ones over the glass fronted bookshelves built in on either side of the fireplace. The fireplace was faced with Mission-style tiles. Kay would be swooning over the pictorial section showing a bas relief scene of pine trees by a lake.

Half-walls and pillars separated the living room from the dining room, which had a nook with more windows over a built in sideboard. Beyond was a closed door that I assumed led to the kitchen.

"Wow," I said, "what a great house."

He grinned at me. "My grandparents built it back in 1912. The materials cost about eleven hundred dollars and he did most of the building himself."

"I imagine that was a chunk of change back then."

"I'm sure it was, but he was a hard worker and so was Grandma. I bet they are laughing their heads off up in heaven over what the place is worth now."

I raised my eyebrows questioningly, and his grin grew wider.

"Some maniac offered me a little over a million for it a couple of weeks ago."

"Zowie." I shook my hand as though it were burned. "You could probably buy half the town I live in for that. If you were in the market for half a town."

"Tempting," he chuckled. "But I'm not selling. I've got everything I need, what would I do with a million bucks? Besides, this place should go to little Natty when I'm gone."

"Kind of fun to turn down a million dollars. I think that might make me feel richer than actually taking the money."

"Exactly! But come in, have a seat. Let those dogs loose so they can sniff around. It's been too long since we had a dog in this house."

I unclipped leashes. Jack gave himself a mighty shake, huge ears flapping, as though he'd been trussed up for hours. "Show off," I told him. He wagged at me, then followed his nose around the room.

Emily Ann walked delicately over to the sofa, stepped up, and curled into the amazingly small circle that is her couch potato shape. "Oh, Emily Ann, come here. Not everyone wants a greyhound on the furniture."

"Leave her be, she's fine." He gestured to a chair upholstered in worn velvet. "Have a seat and tell me what I can do for you. Oh, let me grab those dog cookies first. What can I get you? How about some iced tea?"

"Sounds great."

I settled myself and dropped my bags beside the chair as he hurried to the back of the house. In a few minutes he returned with a glass of tea in each hand. Setting one on the table beside my chair, he reached in his pants pocket and pulled out two bone shaped biscuits. Jack broke off his explorations to come close and give his most winning expression. Mr. Gallagher handed him one of the treats, then sat beside Emily Ann, crossing his legs. He handed her the other biscuit and gave her head a pat.

"I still can't believe how much you look like her."

"You mean the woman in the picture I saw at your grandson's studio? I'm hoping you might be able to tell me more about her. You're right, she does look like me, and I—I have no idea why. I mean, it may just be coincidence, but—"

"But you don't think so. Neither do I. If Eloise had lived, she would still look like an older version of you."

Something cold crawled down my spine. "Eloise?"

"Eloise Abernathy. Well, that was her name when we were in school together. Her husband's name was..." He looked up and to the left, thinking. "Started with a C. Chaney...Chester...no, wait, Chessman, that was it."

I breathed a sigh of relief. I'd been afraid he would say Chelton, my maiden name.

"And her first name was Eloise?"

He nodded.

"That's such a weird coincidence. My mother's name was Eloise too, but she was quite petite and had dark hair. I wonder if they could have been cousins or something. I suppose Eloise might have been a family name."

"Yes, some families do that." He twinkled at me. "I was a little surprised when my son named his son Nate. The third, no less. It's not like we're royalty."

"Your grandson is adorable, by the way."

He nodded. "He's a good boy. And a good photographer. Speaking of which, I had him bring by the whole file of pictures that the one you saw came from."

"There are more?"

"Everything from that shoot. They were never picked up, of course, and I could never bring myself to get rid of them. I guess Eloise's father and sister just couldn't bear to see them." His face sagged into lines of deep sadness. "God, that was such a tragedy. The family never got over it. And I—I, well, I'd been in love with Eloise since I was fourteen. For her to die like that, and her baby and husband too, it was—it was one of the worst things I've ever been through."

I bit my lower lip. "I'm sorry, I don't really know what you're talking about."

107

He raised his eyes to mine. "I forgot. You look so much like her I figured you must somehow know all about it." He swallowed with difficulty, as though a large lump had lodged in his throat. "They were killed at her father's business when the plant exploded." He paused, then added, "Eloise was only nineteen years old."

Oakland, Midcentury

Enough mooning about. He had to get a move on, the taxi was waiting. He walked around the bed to his closet and pulled the door open, clicking on the light. He hated having to leave behind so much of his wardrobe, but he and Joan had agreed they could take only one suitcase each. And he'd have plenty of money to replace all these things.

His shoes were in disarray, not placed neatly in a row as he kept them. His gaze traveled to the back corner where he had stashed the packed suitcase. An involuntary breath rushed into his throat when he saw the bathrobe he had thrown over the case crumpled on the floor.

And the suitcase was gone.

14

I clanged the chain link gate closed behind us. Snapping first Emily Ann's leash, then Jack's, off their collars, I told them, "Please be on your best behavior. We are visitors here, remember."

Jack dashed off on his short legs to chase down some new smells. Emily Ann looked around the dusty bark-covered area then looked up into my face.

"I know, I know, you're used to grass at the dog park," I told her. "Different places, different parks, okay?"

She stuck by my side as I ambled along the path down the center of the long space. Several dogs romped, groups of owners stood chatting, balls and Frisbees sailed through the air. I should have felt right at home, but I could barely take in my surroundings.

Back in the car, tucked into the bag with the baby dress and the family snapshots that Kay had sent me, was what felt to me like—even as I thought it, my brain recoiled from the word—a bomb.

I stopped to look all around. Perhaps Bob had gotten here before me, but I didn't see him. I started walking again, wishing I could immediately share with him what I had learned.

And at the same time I was relieved, not wanting to talk about it to anyone.

I could see the brown leather Keens on my feet walking along the path, Emily Ann's long legs keeping pace, but it was as though the rest of my body was only loosely hinged together, and I wasn't sure where any particular bit of me was in space or what it might be doing.

"Louisa! Hey, Louisa!"

Jack came running back to me with a small black dog by his side, a small black dog with enormous ears. Daphne. I struggled out of my daze. Beside a picnic table near the end of the park, Penny Marquette stood waving at me. "Louisa!" she called again, and began to walk my way. Emily Ann left me to trot over and lead her back.

"Penny, hi, how are you?" I managed to sound quite normal.

"I'm good, how about you? Is Bob with you?"

"He's supposed to meet me here. Neither of us knew how long our appointments would take. What have you been up to?"

We fell into step and strolled up the path, returning to the table she'd been standing by earlier.

The benches looked reasonably clean, so I perched on one. Penny sat beside me.

"Oh, you know, a little field work, a lot of paper work. I just wish I could teach Daphne to file."

I had to laugh. "So it's not enough that she can detect, what do you call them—"

"Accelerants?"

"—an atom of an accelerant in a ton of rubble in a burned out husk of a building, but now you want her to file as well?"

"Damn right. It would be enlightened self-interest on her part. If she filed while I typed and printed reports we could get out of the office in a quarter of the time and she could go play that much sooner."

I nodded. "It's a good plan. Really. Maybe you could open a dog filing school, like the arson detection school you took her to."

She looked thoughtful, considering the idea. "The problem is, most of the guys who have arson dogs think their dogs are way too macho for something like filing. They'd rather do something drastic like hire a secretary than get further training for their dogs."

I shook my head in mock disgust. "There goes another good idea up in—"

I couldn't say the word "smoke." Suddenly my eyes were filled with tears.

"Louisa, what's wrong? Are you all right?"

I nodded, pressing my lips together tightly and holding up a hand. Emily Ann, who had been lying near my feet, rose and put her front paws on the picnic bench. She touched my cheek with her nose. The

111

gesture made the tears spill over. I dashed them away with my fingertips.

"Sorry. I'm okay, really. I—I found out something earlier that—well, I'm a bit shaken."

Her brow furrowed in concern. "Do you want to talk about it?"

"I, um, not yet. It's still too—"

"Louisa! Hi!" Bob's voice. I looked down the path and saw him hurrying in our direction, Jack leaping and bucking in circles around him. I quickly wiped away any lingering tears and reset my expression to welcoming.

Then I saw that he was not alone. The French twist and vintage dress had been replaced with a perfectly cut shoulder length bob and a drapey shirt over jeans so tight that I could only pray the fabric included enough Spandex that the woman could breathe, at least a little.

Adler Beck.

What was Adler Beck doing at a dog park?

And why was she here with Bob?

When they reached us I lifted my face for Bob's kiss, giving him what I hoped looked like a normal smile. It must have been close enough, because he immediately turned to Penny.

"Hey, neighbor," he said in a jovial tone. "How's it going?"

"Good. You?"

"Great. Oh, let me introduce Adler Beck. Adler, this is my neighbor Penny."

Adler shifted the strap of the enormous camera slung over her shoulder so that she could shake hands with Penny. "Hi, nice to meet you."

Penny's lips turned up but her eyes were narrowed. "You too. Which dog is yours?"

"Dog?" Adler looked confused, glancing at Bob as though for reassurance.

"It's a dog park," Penny said, gesturing with her open palm up. "People bring dogs here."

At that moment Daphne ran up and jumped into Penny's lap, as though to say "Ta da!" Her little pink tongue lolled happily out the side of her mouth as she waved her plume of a tail.

"Not me. I don't have a dog," Adler stated.

"We met up over at the university and Adler gave me a ride," Bob explained.

I rather wanted to know why he had not jumped out of the car, thanked her, and watched her drive away, but it would be rude to ask.

"I was in the studio doing some editing, but when Bob said he was coming here I thought I'd come along. I'm always on the lookout for my next subject."

There was a little silence, and I realized Penny and I were both looking at her blankly. Eventually Bob realized it too.

"Adler is a documentary film maker," he explained. "She filmed our trip to Central America a few months ago, when we did the interviews with the shaman who uses medical hypnosis."

Adler smiled modestly. "Yes, it turned out to be quite a trip, didn't it, Bob?"

Something flickered in his eyes, but all he said was, "It was an amazing experience."

I shifted on my picnic bench, remembering that time. While Bob had been in Central America, I had been having my own little adventure that included an English duke traveling incognito and a disguised, solid gold frog. I had been pushed down a stairway and broken my arm, Jack and Emily Ann had been kidnapped. That's when the car I'd been riding in—Bob's car—had been forced off the road into Quarry Pond. I had also knocked out the bad guy, or rather woman, with my cast, which had been extremely satisfying.

None of it had been recorded by a documentarian. I must remember to thank my lucky stars.

"Are you thinking of doing a documentary on dog parks?" Penny asked. "There might actually be an audience for something like that."

The slight emphasis on the last word made my lips twitch.

Adler shrugged. "I usually go for something more...esoteric than cute animals."

Daphne cocked her head, increasing her cuteness level tenfold. Mentally I gave her a thumbs up. Penny was not daunted.

"Oh, but dog parks are about so much more than cuteness. This is where primal instincts are played out in the modern world. Not just the dogs, the humans. They form packs just as much as the dogs do and exhibit quite parallel behavior."

In spite of herself, Adler seemed interested. I added. "That's absolutely true. Wait till you see what happens when two dogs get into a tiff."

Penny laughed and nodded. "Right! Right! As soon as the dogs have settled their differences, the owners start yelling at each other. I've even seen them circling like they're going to attack."

Bob laughed too. "Boy, does that bring back memories," he said, looking at me. I grinned back at him. He turned to Adler. "I actually think they're onto something. If you're interested, we can come back again for you to observe."

She gave him a warm smile. "That would be great, Bob. I have some time next week."

"Oh, but—" Bob looked at me. I waved a dismissive hand.

"Don't worry about me," I said. "I wouldn't want to stand in the way of art."

Penny suddenly lifted Daphne to the ground and stood up. "Who's hungry? Let's take the dogs over to University Street. It's only a couple of blocks away, we can walk."

"What's on University Street?" I asked.

I'm pretty sure Adler rolled her eyes. "Everything."

"Lots and lots of places to eat. And several of them have patios where we can have the dogs. Louisa? Bob?"

"Sounds good to me," Bob said. He looked at Adler. "Want to come?"

"You're going to dinner with your dogs?"

"Of course," I said, rising as well. "That way we know we'll have an interesting companion."

Oakland, Midcentury

Eloise braked hard as the light turned red. Automatically her right arm shot out to hold the baby in place as they both rocked forward, then back. Louisa giggled and banged on her car seat with both hands.

"Oh, you liked that, did you? I need to slow down before I get us both killed." Her teeth ground together. "He'd like that, wouldn't he? He'd get everything and people would feel sorry for him to boot."

The light changed, and in spite of her good intentions to drive safely, her foot stomped on the gas pedal and the car fishtailed as they took off. It had rained earlier, and the taillights of cars in front of her left watery trails of red on the pavement. "What is the matter with these people!" she cried, banging the steering wheel with her fists. "Why are they all such slow pokes? Get out of my way!"

She realized she was screaming. A glance at Louisa showed a startled little face with puckered brows.

"I'm sorry, I'm sorry. I didn't mean to scare you." She took a deep breath and turned her head to smile at Louisa. "I'm all right now. We'll just calmly drive to the plant, and I will calmly walk inside, and calmly tell your father what an absolute swine he is. That—that bastard. That—"

Her vocabulary failed her. She had been too well-brought-up to have a supply of invective at her command. But the lack of words did not stop her mental tirade.

"You lying, scheming son of a bitch." She realized she was practicing what she would say to him. "If it wasn't for Louisa I could kill you right now. I have done nothing but love you, and support you, and do everything I could think of to make you happy, and none of it was one damned bit of good. And now you think you are just going to walk away, is that it? Well, you just go, just go ahead and leave. You will never see Louisa again, I can tell you that, and my father will make sure you never find another job. You...you..." She did not know a vile enough word for him.

By the time she reached the parking lot at her father's business, Eloise was shaking with rage. Her hands ached from her steely grip on the steering wheel. She made a jerky turn into the lot, screeching to a halt in her usual parking space.

She was ready. Carter wouldn't recognize her, the person she had become in the last hour.

The sight of her father's secretary's car parked near the door, next to her husband's Buick, made her pause. She had expected Carter to be the only one here at this hour. The thought of losing her composure in front of Joan was not what she had bargained for.

She had always been intimidated by the other woman. Joan had been her father's personal secretary for two or three years. Eloise remembered the first time they had met, when she was a junior in high school.

She had proudly driven the new Chevy her father had given her for her birthday over after school and parked in the same spot where she was now. She had felt so grown up that day, driving her own car. She loved its gleaming dark blue paint with the white top and white sidewall tires. She remembered how the girls at school had been so envious, not just of the car but of her new clothes. A pink angora sweater tucked into the waistband of a black circle skirt, immaculate saddle shoes, a string of tiny pearls around her neck. She had hopped out of the car and hurried to the building, hoping her father would be free so she could take him for a little spin.

The receptionist's face broke into a beaming smile when she went inside. "Eloise! How nice to see you. Don't you look grown up today. I can hardly believe it's you."

Eloise had grinned back. She had known Florrie Wingate since she was little. "Well, I'm sixteen now. Guess it shows. Is my dad in?"

"He is. Let me ring his secretary to see if he's free. Oh, have you met her? Joan?"

"No, not yet."

"Let me take you back so I can introduce you." Florrie rose and came out from behind her desk. She went to the door that led to the executive offices. "I'm sure this old telephone will be fine without me for a few minutes."

Joan had been speaking on the phone when they reached her office. "That's correct," she was saying, "Tuesday the twenty fifth at four." She looked up as they entered and raised one finger. "That will be fine...Yes...And thank you. Goodbye." She hung up the phone and looked up at Florrie and Eloise. "How can I help you?"

Her tone was polite and business-like. Florrie stood a little straighter. "Joan, I'd like to introduce you to Mr. Abernathy's older daughter, Eloise. Eloise, this is Joan Dexter."

Joan immediately rose and came around the desk to shake Eloise's hand. "It's nice to meet you," she said, the corners of her mouth barely turning up in a smile. "I've heard so much about you from your father."

Eloise had murmured some response as all her earlier euphoria drained away. Joan was small and dainty, with smooth dark hair neatly tucked behind her pretty ears. From her crimson lipstick to her charcoal suit, spotless white blouse and gray pumps, she was the epitome of the perfect personal secretary. She appeared to be only a few years older than Eloise, but Eloise suddenly felt like an unsophisticated child standing there in her clumping saddle shoes.

And now, even though she was grown and married and a mother and wearing a taffeta dress, if she saw Joan tonight, especially if Joan were in Carter's office, Eloise knew that inside she would immediately be sixteen years old again. She gripped the steering wheel hard and slumped in her seat. Her head drooped.

The words she had been rehearsing all the way over here burned in her mouth.

"Oh, Louisa, what am I going to do?" she wailed. She raised her head to look at her little daughter in her car seat.

Baby Louisa was fast asleep.

15

The waiter placed a large, bubbling-hot pizza on a chrome stand in the middle of our table. Artichoke hearts, strips of sweet red onion, and slices of fresh tomatoes nestled into the sizzling cheese. The smell was delicious. Jack and Emily Ann remained lying down, noses quivering, while Daphne rose up on her hind legs and danced in a circle, her dark eyes gleaming.

"Daphne, give it a rest," Penny told her. "You're still eight inches too short to reach the table." With a heartfelt sigh, the little dog lay back down under Penny's chair.

My cell phone rang. Kay's ring. "Excuse me a second, she'll keep calling till I answer," I told the others at the table. Flipping open the little device, I said, "Hi. I can't talk now, the pizza just arrived."

"Ooooh, pizza," she crooned. "Now I want some too. Did you have it delivered to his house? You're all cozy, just the two of you?"

"Um, no. We're in a restaurant with some other people. Let me call you back later."

"Oh, okay. But as soon as you can. I want to hear about your visit with the grandfather."

"Will do. Tell Ed hello for me." I put the phone away and reached for a slice of pizza. "This looks great." I smiled at the group around the table, hoping I looked and sounded normal.

Even though I was not at all certain just what normal was any more.

I almost expected the pizza to have no flavor. I picked up my slice, folded it so all the gooey cheese would stay put and not land on my shirt, and took a big bite. Hot, too hot, registered the roof of my mouth. Delicious! countered my tongue. I took a second bite, which was as good as any I had ever tasted. I ignored the thought about how shallow I must be, to enjoy a pizza after what I had learned that day.

Out of the corner of my eye I noticed that Adler was cutting neat, tiny pieces with her knife and fork.

I took an even bigger bite.

"How is Kay?" Bob asked, when he'd finished his own big bite. For Penny and Adler's benefit he added, "Kay is Louisa's cousin."

"She's fine. I'll call her back later."

"Ohhhh." He smacked himself in the forehead with the hand not holding pizza. "I bet she was calling to find out how your meeting with Mr. Gallagher went today. I completely forgot to ask."

I shook my head. "No problem."

"I'm so sorry. So, how did it go?"

122

"Fine. He's a nice old guy." I hoped that my tone would convey "we'll talk about this later" to Bob.

It didn't.

"Did he recognize the picture? Did you find out anything about that woman?"

Penny added, "Oh, right, you had that appointment with the photographer's grandfather today." I could see her suddenly remember my tears at the park. Her eyes widened and her hand flew to her mouth. No one seemed to notice except me.

Bob turned to Adler. "It was the strangest thing. The photography studio in my neighborhood had some vintage pictures in the window the other day, and one of them looked just like Louisa."

"Really?" Adler cut her eyes in my direction. "How...unusual." She cocked her head and studied me for a moment, then nodded. "Yes, I can see you as— vintage."

Dang, why wasn't Kay here? She would have understood the word vintage to mean old and slugged the woman for me. "It's nothing, just a coincidence." I took another bite of pizza.

"Speaking of vintage," Penny put in quickly, "if you're going to be here long enough, the Alameda flea market is the first Sunday of the month. I bet you'd love it."

"That's right," Bob said. He smiled at me brightly. "Just one of the many things you would like about living here."

Oh god, not now, I groaned inwardly.

"You're thinking of moving here?" Adler's voice had a note of incredulity. "Are you sure you would want to leave your little town?"

She said "your little town" in exactly the same tone my mother used to refer to "your little friends."

I decided not to answer her, but Bob said, "It's under discussion, but I'm trying not to put any pressure on Louisa."

He beamed at me. Maybe we should have a little chat later about what might or might not put pressure on me.

San Francisco, Midcentury

The cabdriver placed the large suitcase near the terminal door as Joan followed him, carrying the matching train case herself. She paid him the fare and a tip, acknowledging his thanks with a cool nod. Tilting her head back, she felt a small thrill at the words "San Francisco International Airport" in huge letters above her; the last time she had been here it had still been the Municipal Airport.

She looked around for a Skycap and saw one hurrying toward her. Relinquishing her train case, she led him to the ticket counter, where he deposited her bags and accepted her tip.

Tipping was one of those niceties that Joan prided herself on getting right. Knowing how and when and how much to tip was one of the million little things that reminded her how far she had come. She was willing to bet that no one else in her hardscrabble family had ever seen a Skycap, let alone tipped one.

A little smile curved her crimson lips. They probably would no longer recognize her, much less a Skycap.

The young man with the crew cut at the counter smiled back at her. "Good evening. How may I help you?"

"My husband and I are flying to New York. He will be here soon. May I leave my bag with you?"

"Of course. Your name?"

"I am Mrs. Randall Chelton."

"Very good, Mrs. Chelton. Would you like to keep your small case with you?"

"Yes, of course."

"The lounge is through that door. When Mr. Chelton arrives, I'll make sure he knows you are here."

"Please tell him if he doesn't see me I will be having a drink in the International Room."

"I certainly will. Have a good flight."

Joan dispensed another nod and tucked her clutch bag under her arm, then picked up the handsome train case. The pair of Wheary bags had cost her nearly a month's wages, but the train case was exactly the right size for this trip.

Her next bags, though—those would be Vuitton.

16

Even though it was still fully dark, when my eyes popped open the next morning I knew I would not be able to go back to sleep. I slipped out of bed, sitting on the edge for a moment to watch Bob. He lay on his side facing me, and the little night light in the hall gave enough illumination to see he was deeply asleep. I thought I saw movement under his eyelids. I wondered what he dreamed about.

Jack rose from his blanket in the corner of the room, stretched and yawned, and moseyed over to me. "Hey, Jack," I whispered, "are you my good boy?" He leaned against the front of my legs and wagged in agreement. "Let me up, sweetie. We'll go find somewhere to watch the sun come up."

The word "go" made him give a little hop.

In a few minutes I was dressed and had batted at my short hair with the brush. A splash of cold water on my face shattered any remaining sleepiness. In the kitchen I poured some orange juice into a small glass, then rummaged in a drawer for a notepad and pen.

"Gone to watch the sun rise, back in a while. Call if you need me." I taped the note to the bathroom mirror, then tiptoed back into the bedroom. Emily Ann had moved onto the bed, exactly where I expected to find her, curling herself into the warm spot I had abandoned. I touched her on the shoulder and she raised her head to blink at me sleepily.

"Come on, sweetie, let's go."

She oozed off the bed and walked into the hallway before stretching. I looked once more at Bob, who had rolled onto his back and was now emitting polite little snores, then followed her.

In the car, I noted the faintest hint of dawn toward the east. I drove away from Bob's house and uphill, looking for the little park I had noticed earlier.

"Do either of you remember what street that was on?" I asked the dogs. They were as clueless as I was. But the predawn streets were blessedly free of traffic, and my trusty old car might have a better memory than mine, because in a few turns something looked familiar, and soon we'd found the park.

It was beyond the crest on the eastern side of the hill. I could see over the rooftops toward the just-visible rolling hills. I pulled the key from the ignition and climbed out, closing the door as quietly as I could. I let the dogs out the back of the car, and we strolled into the park. If I had been alone I would have been nervous about venturing into even a tiny neighborhood park at such a deserted hour. But I was

127

confident that Jack's and Emily Ann's superior senses of hearing and smell would give me early warning of anyone else's presence.

The dogs' calm demeanor reassured me. I settled into a cross-legged perch on the lone picnic table, facing east, awaiting the sun.

Distant car noises filtered through the still air, and in a few minutes I began to hear the waking up noises of birds. Exotic scents wafted by my nose; probably more eucalyptus, and something I didn't recognize that was elusively sweet. I took a deep slow breath, and then another. And let myself begin to think.

Perhaps because I wasn't ready to think about my visit to Mr. Gallagher yesterday, the subject of Bob came rushing to the foreground.

We had known each other nearly a year now. The events of last October, when he'd been kidnapped before my eyes by a blond woman in a snappy red suit, seemed like they had happened no more than a couple of months ago. At that point we had only been acquainted a few days. Going on the run from a two-time murderer had the effect of speeding up the trajectory of our relationship.

Being with Bob had helped me get past the baggage of my long and unhappy marriage. We'd had so much fun together that when he'd been invited to participate in the research project on hypnotic anesthesia at Berkeley early last summer, he had wanted me to come with him. But I couldn't leave Kay without any help in the antique store, and I had just moved into the first house that was all mine. Bob had come alone to California, leaving his car and his dog with me for safekeeping.

I hadn't done too well with his car, but Jack was just fine. And had grown dearer to me every day. My motto has always been, if you're going to lose something, make sure it's the car and not the dog.

I had hoped that the weeks apart would bring clarity to what I wanted regarding Bob. But they hadn't. When we were apart I thought about him much of the time and missed his conversation, his laugh, his kiss. At the same time I relished being alone in my house with only the dogs for company. Their undemanding companionship felt just right. I loved being able to leave a book open on the kitchen counter in the evening and having it still there the next day. I loved having no one else to clean up after or cook for. No one else's feelings to consider or desires to consult.

I loved knowing the toilet seat would always be in the position I preferred.

That's so selfish, I thought. Isn't it wrong to live just for myself? But I couldn't help feeling I had done enough taking care of someone else's ego for six lifetimes.

Bob was *nothing* like Roger. Or if he was, I couldn't see it. Yet.

Mentally I walked away from my internal debate and gazed out at the growing light in the east. Hills and trees were now sharply defined silhouettes, and the streaky clouds above were beginning to emit a pink glow.

I had felt such a lurch of happiness when I parked my car in front of Bob's house a few days ago, and he'd coming running out the front door, jumped over the steps, and grabbed me. At the same time I remembered having to force myself to stop driving toward Canada instead of California.

I had no doubt that Bob loved me. But I also had no sense of having come home since I arrived here.

I thought of the stab of disappointment I had felt yesterday when he'd forgotten to ask me about my visit with Mr. Gallagher. On the other hand, he'd been busy all afternoon, and he had that woman with him.

Yeah. That Woman.

I did not like her.

At least Penny had deflected the conversation from the picture of the woman who looked like me. I didn't mind a bit if Penny knew what I had found out, but I hated the thought of Adler learning anything about me.

The last person I had disliked this much had pushed me downstairs and broken my arm, kidnapped my dogs, and dumped them by a freeway. I flexed my newly-healed bone.

After we returned home yesterday evening, Bob had gotten a phone call about the research project, and then another, and I had escaped to bed before he remembered to ask me again what I had learned.

Unbidden tears welled up and spilled down my cheeks. I had gotten used to being the last thing my husband considered, but it hurt to feel that Bob was treating me the same way.

"Dammit," I muttered, feeling in my pocket to see if by some miracle a tissue was lurking there. No such luck. I sniffled. "Stop it. Just stop it," I commanded.

Jack put his feet on the picnic bench and looked at me, his tail moving in a worried little wag.

"I'm okay, Jack. Really."

The rim of the sun slid into view, gilding the clouds that dotted the sky. I got down from the picnic table.

"Come on, you guys. Let's go find that little bakery I saw the other day." I gave one last sniffle and smiled at their eager faces. "I'll get a pastry and a cup of tea and call your Auntie Kay, and after that maybe Bob will be awake."

Oakland, Midcentury

Carter flew down the stairs and flung himself off the porch, tripping and nearly falling but catching his balance and racing on to the cab. He yanked the door open and fell inside.

"Take me back to where you picked me up. And fast, man, as fast as you can."

17

When I walked into Bob's house I was greeted by the smell of coffee. I unleashed the dogs and carried my bakery bag to the kitchen. No one there, but voices wafted in from the back yard.

I opened the back door and the dogs dashed out to greet Penny and Bob, who were lounging at the table, coffee mugs in hand, talking earnestly.

"I brought treats," I announced, holding up the bag.

Bob jumped up and met me with a kiss. "You're back! How was the sunrise?"

"Gorgeous." I handed him the bag and leaned over to pet Daphne, who was sniffing my shoes. "Hey, cutie pie, there are dog treats in that bag as well as people food." Straightening, I said, "Let me go grab a cup of tea. Do we have napkins? Be right back."

When I returned, I brought the bag of photos with me and laid it on the table by my place. I pulled the dog cookies out of the bag. "Help yourselves, I got four or five kinds of Danish. Hey dogs, who wants a—"

No need to finish that sentence. All three dogs flew to me and sat, looking expectant. I handed each a treat, and settled into my own chair as they happily crunched away.

"These look great," said Penny. "Did you go to Katrina's?"

I nodded. "I got a Danish and a cup of tea, and after one bite I went back and got more to bring home. I was afraid they'd all disappear in the time it took me to eat that one."

Penny laughed. "They could have, too. You are quickly learning our ways here."

Bob took a bite of the blueberry cream cheese version. "Mmmm," he moaned. "I fear you have introduced me to a new vice."

"You'll have to be an early riser to feed your addiction," Penny warned him. "Katrina really does sell out every morning."

Bob is not the morning person that I am. He heaved a sigh. "It's probably just as well. Think what daily Danishes would do to my budget. Of course, if Louisa *does* stay, she could become a regular."

He gave me a hopeful look. I ignored it. A little silence fell. We nibbled on pastries.

After a few moments, Penny said, "Louisa, I wanted to apologize."

"What for?" I asked in surprise.

"Oh, I felt like I put my foot in it at the pizza place. I could see you didn't want to talk in front of that woman. About your picture."

It seemed tactless to point out that Bob was the one who had run with that topic. "It was nothing," I assured her. "Though you're right, I can't say I've really taken to Adler."

Bob looked astonished. "Really? Why?"

Penny's eyes met mine for just a moment, then we both looked down, neither of us able to come right out and say, because she's a bitch. "Oh, just chemistry, I guess. And I didn't really appreciate some of the things she said at the party, while I was waiting for you."

"But—but you weren't even in that group."

No, but I have ears like a bat, I thought crossly. "True. But speaking of the photo—" I took a deep breath. "I—I guess I should bring you both up to speed on what I learned yesterday. Bob and I never got a chance to talk last night," I added to Penny.

"So you did find out more?" he asked.

I nodded. "I found out a lot. And—well, some of it has me reeling."

In his living room the day before, Mr. Gallagher had taken the photo of the young woman with the baby between his hands and smiled at it tenderly. "Eloise. And her baby. She was so proud of that child."

"I don't suppose you remember the baby's name?"

"Of course I do! It was, um—" He frowned. "Don't you hate it when that happens? Two seconds ago I could have told you. Well, it will come back to me. If I suddenly blurt out a name, that'll be it."

"That happens to me all the time. Not being able to recall something, I mean. I don't usually blurt out names."

"Wait till you're my age," he chuckled. "Anyway, I do remember the day this was taken like it was yesterday. It was in the fall, October I think. My father had made the appointment for pictures of the Chessman family. The name had sounded vaguely familiar to me but I hadn't pinned it down. He was in the studio setting up, and I was out front in the reception area when the door opened and Eloise walked in. I'd only seen her a couple of times since graduation, and I thought I had gotten over her, but as soon as she walked in I knew I hadn't. If she had been single I'd have asked her out then and there, but she was carrying a baby. That's when I remembered seeing the wedding announcement in the paper, and that she had married a guy named Chessman."

"Was her husband with her?"

"He came ten or fifteen minutes later. Eloise was always early for everything. I was glad since it gave us a chance to catch up. We went on back to the studio and started with pictures of just Eloise and the baby. That little imp had just started to crawl and she was into everything. And whenever Eloise picked her up, she went for those buttons on the front of that dress. She was determined to eat them. Dad was shooting with the Deardorff, the big studio camera, but I had my Leica and was grabbing random shots. I remember I had a feeling that I might not see Eloise again."

"Really?"

"Oh, it wasn't a premonition or anything. But she was married now, with a baby, and her dad was this really successful businessman. They had lots of money. We didn't. It just felt like our lives were going down two different paths. Maybe if I had gotten up the nerve in high school to ask her out...but I hadn't. Anyway, after about twenty minutes or so her husband showed up."

He fell silent. Jack rose from where he had eaten his biscuit and walked over to the sofa to lean against the old man's legs. Mr. Gallagher gave him a pat.

"He was—impatient. Polite, but clearly didn't want to be there. The way he spoke to Eloise was, well, cold. The only time I saw him with a real smile was when the baby crawled over to him and sat on his foot. I remember being so excited when I caught that moment with my Leica, the baby looking up at her father and the smile on his face as he looked down. I planned to include it in the packet with the more formal shots, maybe even frame it for Eloise. I knew she would love it. But she never got to see it."

"So the—the tragedy happened soon after?"

He nodded. "Days later. Not more than a couple of weeks."

He leaned forward and picked up a thick manila envelope from the coffee table. I'd been so focused on him I hadn't noticed it before. He unwound the red string that held it closed and peered inside. In a moment he pulled out a yellowed newspaper clipping and handed it across to me.

Four people are missing and presumed dead as the result of an explosion and fire at the Abernathy Printing Company in Oakland on Tuesday night.

The victims are Carter Chessman, 29, vice president of sales for the company; his wife Eloise Abernathy Chessman, 19, and their daughter Louisa, 6 months; and Joan Dexter, 32, the company's executive secretary.

The explosion and fire destroyed the printing plant. Because the fire started so quickly, firefighters were unable to save any of the structure. Several vehicles in the adjacent parking lot were also destroyed, including delivery trucks belonging to the company and automobiles registered to Mr. and Mrs. Chessman and Miss Dexter.

The cause of the explosion has not yet been determined. According to printing foreman Aloysius Cromwell, the plant did not use volatile materials or store explosives in its warehouse. However, the company has been working with the Bank of America to implement a new type of magnetic printing on checks. "Maybe it was something to do with that," Cromwell stated.

Because of the intensity of the fire, no bodies have been recovered. But police have determined that the burned-out cars in the parking lot were registered to the assumed victims.

According to Mrs. Florence Wingate, 53, receptionist for the firm, Mr. Chessman sometimes worked late after the rest of the staff had left for the day. "Joan, Miss Dexter, must have stayed late to help him," she stated. "I imagine Mrs. Chessman brought the baby with her when she came to the office that evening. I believe they had plans to go to dinner when they left the plant."

Frank Abernathy, owner of the business, was unavailable for comment.

Investigations into the cause of the explosion continue.

Now, sitting in Bob's back yard, I handed the same yellowed piece of newsprint across the table to Penny. Bob scooted his chair next to hers so they could both read it.

"My god," Bob said when he finished, "that must have been a hell of an explosion."

"Do you know if they ever determined a cause?" Penny asked. I shook my head.

"According to these follow up articles, apparently not." I pulled three more pieces of paper from the envelope and handed them over. I didn't need to read them again, I knew only too well what they said.

ARSON SUSPECTED IN PRINTING PLANT DEATHS

Investigators for the Oakland Fire and Police Departments have now named the explosion and fire at the Abernathy Printing plant "suspicious." No definite cause has been determined, but an unnamed spokesman for the Fire Department said this week that the magnitude of the explosion indicates that it was caused deliberately.

The spokesman went on to say, "There is no evidence that the deaths of four people was in any way planned. It is more likely that they were in the wrong place at the wrong time. But the nature of the chemicals used for printing would not normally be volatile enough to cause such a conflagration."

Investigations will continue until a definite cause has been determined.

ABERNATHY UNDER INVESTIGATION

Frank Abernathy, owner of the Abernathy Printing Company, was questioned by police Friday after a customer, the Bank of America, revealed "financial irregularities" in their dealings with the company.

According to a bank spokesman, Abernathy's company recently closed a deal to implement a new type of ink for printing bank checks. The ink contains magnetic elements that will allow faster processing on checks. The Bank of America paid a "substantial sum" for startup of the project. Bank officials declined to name the exact sum.

Financial records for the printing company were destroyed in the explosion and fire that consumed the business Tuesday night. However, three local banks reportedly cashed checks drawn on the Abernathy account earlier on Tuesday. The checks were made out to "Cash" and signed by Abernathy. The sum of the checks reportedly exceeded $250,000.

Bank of America claims that the money in question was their upfront payment.

Abernathy refused to speak to reporters. According to attorney Tyler Finn, a partner at the Sethton, Gamble, Finn and Locksley law firm in San Francisco, "Mr. Abernathy and his accountants are working to clear up all financial questions that have come about because of the fire. Mr. Abernathy was out of town at the time of the tragedy. Because of the extent of the loss of records it may take some time to get a complete picture."

In response to questions about the deaths that occurred in the explosion, Finn stated, "Mr. Abernathy is grieving the loss of his daughter, granddaughter and son-in-law, as well as his personal secretary who had worked for him for some years. He will not be speaking to the press regarding their deaths."

Though no arrests have been made in the possible arson case or the alleged financial irregularities, a police spokesman indicated that the investigation is ongoing.

"Mr. Gallagher told me that the case faded from the public eye after this. Something else came along to make the front page, I guess. He didn't know for sure, but he thought they never did figure out the cause of the explosion. He didn't know anything more about the money."

Bob looked thoughtful. "Louisa," he started, then stopped.

"What?"

"Well...I don't understand why this would have you reeling, as you said earlier. I mean, I know it was a horrible tragedy, and I can see that you would feel more strongly about it since the woman who was killed looked so much like you. But still, she was a stranger, and it was a long time ago."

"There's more."

"Ah."

I pulled another piece of newsprint from the envelope. It was large and had been folded several times in order to fit. I unfolded it and handed it across the table. "Their obituaries. You don't have to read it all, just take a look at the pictures."

They obeyed. "This looks like the same picture we saw at the studio," Penny said, pointing to the clipping.

"It is. Mr. Gallagher said that Eloise's younger sister called and asked if they could supply pictures to the paper, since these had been taken a few days earlier. The—the husband's picture is from them too. I don't know where they got the picture of the other woman, the secretary. Okay, now take a look at this."

I pulled from the packet one of the family photos that Kay had sent to me. It was a black and white snapshot taken at my third birthday, me blowing out three candles with the help of two-year-old Kay. My Aunt Poppy was next to Kay, her face glowing with laughter. Standing a few feet away with his arm over her shoulder were my parents; she was looking up into his face. I looked at the photo once more before handing it to Bob.

They glanced at it, then did nearly identical double takes and looked more closely. Penny raised her eyes to mine, her expression shocked.

Bob sputtered, "But—but..."

I nodded. "Those are my parents standing off to the side. Well, at least I guess that is my father. But the woman I thought was my mother—wasn't."

The face of the dark-haired woman standing next to my father was clearly that of the secretary, Joan Dexter.

Oakland, Midcentury

Eloise narrowed her eyes and squared her jaw. All right, so be it. If both Carter and Joan were there, all the better. She would march in, tell Carter to get his damned suitcase out of her car, and march out again. No tears, no recriminations. Just the most sneering look she could manage. And then she and Louisa would drive away into their new life.

"I'll be right back," she said softly to the sleeping child. She leaned over and smoothed back a golden curl, then gently kissed her child's brow.

18

"Louisa, are you *sure?*" Bob demanded.

Before I could make even one of the remarks that came to mind, Jack jumped to his feet and flew toward the gate at the side of the yard, barking fiercely. He gave a mighty leap, but his Basset ancestry prevented him from being able to jump a six-foot-tall barrier.

"What the—?" Bob said. He rose and hurried over to Jack, who was barking and leaping against the gate. Taking Jack by the collar, he pulled him down. "What's the matter, boy?"

Still hanging on to the collar, he reached over and unlatched the gate. When he pulled it open I saw a woman halfway down the path along the side of the house, hurrying away.

"Hey!" Bob shouted. She stopped and turned.

"Hi, Bob."

"Adler, hi." His tone turned cordial. What's up?"

Penny and I exchanged a long look. "I don't believe this," she muttered.

"Hide the pastries," I muttered back. She snickered.

Adler sidled back to the gate. "I was hoping you'd be home," she smiled at Bob. "I—I heard voices from back here so I came around."

Could she possibly be unaware that we just saw her trying to sneak away?

Bob let go of Jack's collar and held the gate open wider. "Come on in. We were just having breakfast. Can I get you anything? Coffee?"

She strolled over to the table and sat down, putting her camera and some other piece of equipment on the ground beside the chair she had chosen. Smiling over her shoulder at Bob, she said, "I would absolutely *love* a cup of your coffee."

He lit up with a big smile. "Great, coming right up. Sugar? Cream?"

"Just the tiniest dollop of cream, please."

"Can do. Louisa, Penny, can I bring anyone anything?"

We both shook our heads. He hurried off to the house. As one we turned to gaze at Adler. Emily Ann rose from her spot in the shade and came to stand beside me. She too stared at the newcomer. A moment later, Daphne jumped up into Penny's lap and turned to stare as well. Jack contented himself with settling down on top of my feet with a groan. I let the silence spin out a little too long before I spoke.

"So, Adele, did you hear anything good out there?"

She nodded, unfazed. "It was pretty interesting. Are these the clippings?"

She reached out to pick up the obituaries. Of its own accord, my hand whipped out and slapped the old piece of newsprint back onto the table.

She shrugged. "I'm an investigative journalist, Louisa. I hardly think I'll have trouble finding these articles."

"I thought you were a documentary filmmaker," Penny said. "I wish you'd make up your mind."

"The two go hand in hand. Actually."

My lips twitched as I squelched an involuntary smile. She sounded like a snotty fourteen-year-old with that 'actually.'

In a moment she added, "Some things aren't very hard to investigate though." She gave me a big smile.

I looked back at her steadily, wondering what she had unearthed about me. Or what Bob might have told her. Before I could say anything aloud, he returned, carefully carrying a coffee mug.

"Here you go," he said, setting it in front of Adler. "One cup o' coffee with a tiny dollop of cream."

She smiled up at him as she picked up the mug. After a tiny sip she set it down again. "Mmmm, delish, thanks."

"So to what do we owe the honor?" Bob said as he returned to his chair.

"We need to go over the interview questions for the next radio show," Adler replied.

Bob frowned at her, puzzled. "Did we have an appointment that I've forgotten? I'm really sorry, now isn't a good time. We were—in the middle of something."

145

She didn't miss a beat. "Oh, I'm sorry, did I get the time wrong? It's just, well, I'm not sure when we can meet if not now. But that's okay." She stood.

I pushed my chair back. "Penny, how about we take these dogs for a walk and let Bob get on with his job."

"Great!" She got to her feet, spilling Daphne off her lap.

Bob's face fell a little. "You girls don't have to go."

"That's okay. You might as well meet now that Adler is here."

I rose to my feet, walked around the table and kissed the top of Bob's head. "I'll be back later. Call me if you need anything. Maybe we'll take the dogs to the park or something. Don't work too hard." Patting my thigh, I called, "Emily Ann! Jack! Want to go out?"

The O word galvanized them into action. They ran across the yard and into the house, along with Daphne. Penny and I followed more slowly.

Behind me, I heard Bob say, "Okay, remind me which interview is next. The soccer player or the woman who had the baby?"

"Woman with baby. Soccer player is in two weeks."

"Shoot, I thought he was first. I've been working on his set of questions instead of hers."

"Good thing I came by then."

Inside, I grabbed my purse from the front hall closet.

"Do you have to be anywhere this morning?" I asked Penny, who shook her head.

"Free as a bird."

"Then come on." I clipped leashes on the dogs, she clipped one on Daphne, and we headed out the front door toward the car. I opened the back hatch and all three dogs hopped in. Penny and I climbed into our seats and buckled up. "Let's get out of here."

Oakland, Mid Century

The taxi took the last corner and raced toward the printing plant. Carter strained forward, willing the vehicle to go faster. There was a flash of light and an enormous boom. The ground juddered beneath them.

"Hey, what was that?" the taxi driver exclaimed. "Was that a earthquake?"

The taxi crested the hill and skidded into the parking lot, screeching to a halt. Carter flung open his door.

"Call the fire department!" He stumbled out of the car and ran toward the burning building. The tires squealed behind him as the taxi fled.

The building was already an inferno. Whatever Joan had hidden in the warehouse had done its job all too well. They had parked their cars close to the building in hopes that they would be destroyed, so that no one would question their disappearance. Joan's was already ablaze, and as he ran, his own exploded. He threw himself to the ground, then lurched back to his feet.

Eloise's car was parked four rows away from the building, the space she had always considered hers.

She said parking there gave her luck. He couldn't see if she was in the car, so he began to run again. But in a few steps he saw that the driver's seat, backlit by the raging fire, was empty. His steps slowed.

And then he heard it. The terrified wail of a baby.

19

"So, where are we going, anyway?" Penny asked as we waited for a light to turn green. I blinked.

"Gosh, I don't really know. I just needed to get out of the house."

"And away from that woman." She gave a decisive nod. "She is a piece of work, isn't she?"

"Do you think she's after Bob?"

She cocked her head, considering. The light turned green and the line of traffic began to move.

"I'm not sure," she finally said. "I didn't get so much of a sexual vibe as...I guess maybe a power vibe."

"Hmm. That may be it."

"Have you seen how she acts around other men?"

I shook my head. "No, but I saw her with several women at the party the other night. She was definitely in control of the group as soon as she joined it. Before even, as soon as one of them saw her enter the house."

"Maybe she just has a really healthy ego. It would take a lot of confidence to make documentaries."

"True. I could be letting personal antipathy cloud my judgment."

"Then we both are. I do not trust her."

I thought about Adler as I drove, then said, "The implication of a documentary is that it shows the facts. She strikes me as the kind of person who would present so-called facts any way she wants."

"Which ties in with the journalist thing too. People believe what they read, and who bothers to check on the credentials of a reporter?"

We were silent for a few minutes, then Penny said, "Did we ever decide where we're going?"

"I think I need to do some research. In the obituaries—"

"Which I grabbed off the table, by the way."

I took a quick look at her before returning my gaze to the road. "You did? Brilliant."

She gave a snicker. "Well, after the way you practically slapped her hand when she reached for them, I kind of thought maybe you didn't want her to have them. Just a hunch, you know."

"I knew you were smart."

"Say, how much money did that article say was missing?" She opened her purse and pulled out several pieces of newsprint.

"I think—was it a couple hundred thousand?"

"Here it is. 'Reportedly exceeded $250,000' it says. Hmmm."

"What?"

"Oh, I'm just wondering what that would equate to in today's dollars. Hang on." She put back the articles and pulled out her phone, tapping away at the tiny screen. "Wow."

"Wow? How much wow?"

"That equates to over two and a quarter million today."

"Good heavens. So...a large enough sum to be worth taking risks for."

"Apparently they thought it was. So what are we looking for in the obituaries?"

"My mo—Eloise's and—and Carter's..." I stopped, frowning. "I really don't know what to call them. I'm ninety-nine percent certain that the woman in the picture was in fact my mother, and I was that baby. I know for sure that was a young version of my father in the picture unless he had an identical twin, which I know he didn't because I grew up around his actual brother, my Uncle Bill. If there had been a twin, someone would have let it slip. Or my cousin Kay would have weaseled it out of her dad and then told me. And his name was not Carter Chessman, it was Randy Chelton."

"So barring the unlikely contingency that a guy who looked exactly like your father also had a baby named Louisa exactly your age, I think we can safely assume these are your real parents."

"But I've spent nearly sixty years thinking the other woman was my mother. And that *her* name was Eloise."

151

"To be fair, if she raised you then she was also your mother, like any adoptive mother would be."

"But—"

"But what?"

"Oh, nothing." This didn't seem like the time or place to say that I had grown up feeling as though I had no mother at all. If I even tried I was sure my younger self would begin to wail and cry in self-pity and I would probably wreck the car. "I—I just don't know what to call anyone."

"Then for now, why don't we gain a little distance by just referring to them as Carter and Eloise? And Joan. That would probably be the least confusing."

I nodded. "Good idea."

"Are they still alive? I don't think you said."

"No. He died about a year and a half ago, and she—she committed suicide not long after."

"Oh my gosh. I'm so sorry. Wow."

"Yeah."

We drove in silence for a few minutes, until Emily Ann poked the back of my neck with her cold nose and I gave a shaky laugh. "Hey, you dog. Don't distract the driver."

Penny reached over the seat and gave Emily Ann a pat. "And so where are we going?"

I had to laugh. It was good to be around someone who stayed focused. "Wherever I can find out anything about any of the names in those obituaries."

"Okay, so the library. We can do some research online, but I hate doing serious searching on my phone. And we may need more than what Google can give us."

"And the only thing my phone does is make phone calls. At least as far as I know."

"Okay, how about this. Let's go to the dog park for real and let these guys play for an hour. Then we can take them back to my house and leave them there to snooze and gossip while we go to the library. If Adler's car is gone by then we can make Bob come along to help."

"You think she'll be gone in an hour?"

"Well...I hope so. Anyway, I can at least use my phone to find out which library branch has old newspapers on microfilm, for the stuff that isn't online."

"Perfect. How do I get to the dog park from here?"

She looked around, then nodded. "Take a left at that light up there, then another left in a couple of blocks. It's not very far away at all."

I saw Bob as soon as he walked in the door, and stood up and waved. He looked around, raised his hand when he saw me, and threaded his way through the crowded space. I was relieved that he was alone. I'd been half afraid that Adler would still be with him.

"This is a change," he said, looking around. "I don't think I've ever actually met you in a bar before."

"This one looked cooler than the ones at home. And I thought some wine might not come amiss, even though it's early."

It was in fact nearly five o'clock. Our researches had predictably taken far longer than we had expected. Penny had insisted on a lunch break around one, which was fortunate or the single glass of dry Riesling I had nearly finished would have left me semi-comatose.

He leaned across the tiny table where my wine glass rested and gave me a kiss. "Did you have a good day?"

"Mmm, it was interesting. Let's get you something to drink and I'll tell you. How about yours?"

He nodded. "We got quite a bit done. Adler—"

He broke off at the arrival of our waitress. She looked more like a stay-at-home mom in her casual clothes than someone who would be serving drinks in a hip bar. "What can I get you?" she asked Bob.

"I'll take a fifty fifty Manhattan." He looked over at my glass. "And another glass of wine for the lady."

She nodded and glided away.

"That sounded sophisticated," I commented. He gave a little shrug.

"Oh well, when in Rome. Where are the dogs, anyway?"

"They're at Penny's house, having a play date with Daphne."

He raised an eyebrow in amusement. "Our dogs have play dates?"

"Yup. When in Rome."

The hubbub of the place filled the silence between us while we waited for the waitress to return. She arrived with a small tray and whipped a cocktail napkin onto the table, then Bob's drink. My wine glass was settled in front of me and she picked up the empty one. Then a shallow little bowl of herbed nuts went on the table and she whisked away.

Bob picked up his glass and held it in my direction. "Cheers."

I clinked my glass against his and took a sip, set it down. "So what were you about to say about Adler?"

He looked blank for a moment, then shook his head. "I don't even remember. Probably just that we're much better prepared to do the next interview."

"That's good. If you're confident that will help the person you're interviewing to be confident as well."

"Good point. And I'm a lot clearer on the direction Adler wants the conversation to go."

I shifted on my chair. "Wouldn't that be up to the person you're talking to? The—the interviewee?"

"Well, sure. But Adler says the piece will come across with more authority if you start out knowing the direction you want to take it." He paused to take a sip of his drink, then added. "She's an excellent director."

"I bet she is." I did my best to keep the dry tone out of my voice.

"But tell me about your day. What did you find out? Oh, by the way, did you take those newspaper clippings with you?"

"Yes, I have them. Did you want to read them again?"

"Well, I didn't get to actually read the obituaries. And Adler was asking me what it was all about."

I stared at him. "You didn't tell her, did you?"

"I sort of sketched the outline of what the old guy told you. Why?"

"Why?" I swallowed hard. "Why would you tell her anything about me?"

"What do you mean? You're my girlfriend, she's a colleague. I talk about you. What's wrong with that?"

"Bob, I have just found out that my whole life was based on a lie. I am feeling more than a little emotional about all this. Adler is a stranger with whom I have no connection, and furthermore she is a journalist." I looked into his eyes. "You know how I hated all the publicity after my husband died, and then again when—when you got kidnapped."

"And when that madwoman tried to kill you, and the thing that happened with the duke. I know, you've been through a lot. But Adler wasn't being a journalist, she was just being my friend."

Yeah, right. "Maybe she was, Bob. But she's not my friend. Please, don't talk about me with her. Or anyone else for that matter. I'm still sorting out how I feel about all this—deception."

"Of course I won't." He gave me a warm smile. "If that's what you want."

"That is definitely what I want."

"All right then. My lips are sealed. I had no idea you felt this way. I'm sorry."

"I know. I haven't yet figured out just how I do feel."

"I want you to like it here, Louisa. You know I want you to stay."

I swallowed. "I know. I'm thinking about it all the time. It's a big decision on so many levels."

His eyes were warm, and he reached across the table to cover my hand with his. "Of course. So, what did you find out today?"

"Well, Penny and I went to the library. Basically we were trying to find out anything about any of the names mentioned in the articles."

"Did you find anything?"

"More obituaries, mostly. My—Eloise's father, Frank, died in 1961 at the age of sixty. His only surviving relative was his daughter Leonora. His wife Lois had died in 1942. Maybe when Leonora was born, the math is about right."

"Is she still around? Leonora?"

"We couldn't find an obituary, but that doesn't really mean anything. Lots of women still take their husband's name, and obituaries don't always give the maiden name. And if she married young, like back in the Fifties or Sixties, it's almost a certainty she would have assumed her husband's name."

"True."

"I didn't get married until the mid-Seventies, and even then I never gave a second thought to taking Roger's last name." If only I'd had second thoughts about everything to do with Roger. "Also, people don't stay put. She could have moved anywhere. Anyway, we didn't find an obituary for her. But we did find something else."

"What?"

"Apparently the police thought she might have done it."

He frowned. "Done what?"

"Blown up the building."

Oakland, Midcentury

"All right, let's go over this again." Detective Lawrence Reising of the Oakland Police closed the door and crossed to the table where Lennie sat, her hands gripping each other so hard the knuckles were bloodless. He pulled out the chair opposite her and turned it around, straddled the seat and crossed his arms on the back.

"Go over what? I've told you everything I know," Lennie Abernathy said. Her voice quavered and she pressed her lips tightly together.

"Oh, I bet you know something we haven't heard yet," Reising said mildly. "How about if we start with where your sister is?"

Lennie stared at him in confusion. "What do you mean? My—my sister is dead."

He nodded judiciously. "Maybe she is, maybe she isn't. We didn't find her body."

Lennie jumped to her feet. The heavy wooden chair fell backward with a crash. "She was blown up! My sister was—blown up."

Her face crumpled. She stood defenseless, arms hanging straight at her sides, as she fought to take in enough air to fuel her sobs. Reising stood, walked around the table, picked up the chair.

"Sit."

Lennie collapsed into the chair. Her head went down onto her arms on the table as she continued to weep. "She's dead. My sister is dead."

Reising let her cry for a few minutes, then asked, "When did you last see her?"

"I told you, we had dinner at their house last week. Tuesday night. I've *told* you that." Lennie raised her head and sat back in the chair. Her slumped shoulders looked defeated.

"So you and your old man had dinner with your sister and brother-in-law on Tuesday. By midnight on Friday, your father's printing plant had been bombed and burned to the ground. Three cars were in the parking lot, excuse me, the remains of three cars were in the parking lot, and three people are missing. And so is a whole lot of money."

Lennie's face turned to stone. "Four people."

"What?"

"Four people are missing. D—dead. Louisa is gone too."

Reising looked away, in spite of himself. He didn't much care what the hell was going on with this family, but the thought of a six-month-old baby dying that way...

Even a jaded old cop could feel something about that. He took a breath and looked back at Lennie.

"That's right. That baby is gone. And if you had anything to do with it, then the electric chair is too good for you, even if you are just a kid yourself."

Lennie shook her head slowly. The look she gave Reising was almost one of pity. "I loved them. I did not kill them."

"Oh yeah? I hear you didn't love Joan Dexter, your father's secretary. And I also hear that you told at least two people you were afraid something was going to happen at the printing plant. So if you didn't blow the place up, it sounds like maybe you know who did. Give me a name so we can both go home."

Her sigh came from the soles of her feet. "I don't know anything."

20

The magazines in the silent waiting room were glossy and new. No seven-year-old *Good Housekeeping* issues here, nor even a recent *Martha Stewart*. The latest editions of the *Robb Report, Global Living, BBC History* and *Atomic Ranch* lay fanned in an arc across the surface of the coffee table in front of the comfortable settee where I waited. The receptionist had given me the customary questionnaire on a clipboard to fill out, though instead of the more familiar piece of chipboard or plastic, the clipboard was a heavy, beautifully polished slab of teak with inlaid designs cut from some kind of pearlescent shell. I glanced at the questionnaire, but set it aside without addressing any of the questions.

I was hoping to ask questions, not answer them.

After several silent minutes, I picked up the *Robb Report* and flipped through its slick pages. I soon realized why it seemed familiar. My husband had subscribed to it for his office. I laid it down again. My need for information on superyachts was minimal, and the other item that had caught my eye, a new kind of refrigerator that included a built-in camera to take pictures of the contents every time the door closed, would also be an unlikely purchase. Apparently this incessant photography allowed the lucky refrigerator owner access to the photos through a linked smartphone so they might pick up any needed groceries on the way home.

Roger would have loved it, not that he had ever stopped for groceries on his way home. Bob would definitely stop for groceries, but he didn't need a smartphone to figure out how to make a grocery list.

As for me, I would have to acquire a smartphone before I shelled out for the fridge.

A door opened to my right. "Mrs. McGuire? I'm Dr. Wingate. Won't you come in?"

I stood and walked the few steps to the door. The woman waiting there was about my age and height. Her gray hair was cut even shorter than mine and stuck up in bold spikes. Her simple black linen tunic and slacks were accessorized with bold, brightly colored beads at neck and wrists. Two-inch-long red earrings dangled from her lobes, and her hand-painted shoes were masterpieces of colorful abstractionism. I looked her up and down and smiled.

"Wow," I said. "I want to look just like you when I grow up."

She laughed, gesturing me into her office. "You can! I used to wear suits, can you believe it? I had a

162

whole closetful of suits in light gray and dark gray and for crazy days I switched to charcoal. Then one day I went to a street fair with my friend and she made me try on all this bold chunky loud stuff, and I loved it and bought everything. And that afternoon this guy who takes pictures for his blog of old ladies he thinks are stylish came up and photographed me. So I went home and burned all my suits. Have a seat. Tell me why you're here."

Her office had a beautifully-proportioned midcentury teak desk in one corner, but she turned to the two comfortable arm chairs near the full-height French doors that were opened to reveal a shallow balcony. A small table between the chairs held a pitcher of ice water, two crystal tumblers, and one of those ridiculous Kleenex box covers that dispense the tissues from the nose. She gestured to the chair on the right as she seated herself in the other. I sat and placed my bag on the floor.

"Dr. Wingate, I really appreciate your making the time to see me. I'll try not to be too long. I—I am trying to piece together the facts of something that happened a long time ago, and I ran across a name similar to yours in an old newspaper article."

"Intriguing."

"Are you by any chance related to a Florence Wingate who worked in a printing plant in Oakland back in the Fifties?"

"I sure am. She was my grandmother. I was named for her."

I breathed a sigh of relief. "Oh, good. If you hadn't been related I'm sure you would have thought I was nuts."

"It would take more than that. After all, I am a psychiatrist. I have very high standards in nutsiness."

I loved the twinkle in her dark brown eyes. "Well, here's the story. I'm visiting from the Midwest, staying in Berkeley with a friend, and by chance the other day I passed a display of vintage photos in a shop window. This one stopped me in my tracks."

I picked up my bag and pulled out the picture of Eloise and baby Louisa, taking a quick look at it before handing it to her. She studied it, then looked up at my face, then back to the photo. After a few minutes' scrutiny she said, "You were the baby, weren't you."

I nodded. "I'm pretty sure I was. I still have the dress. I found it among my parents' things after they died a couple of years ago."

"You look a lot like your mother."

"Yes. Except—I had never seen this woman before I found the picture. Tell me, did your grandmother ever talk about the explosion that destroyed the printing plant where she worked?"

Her attention sharpened. "My grandmother, no. I only remember one time, when I was about eleven. She was reading something in the newspaper and I found her in tears. I asked her what was wrong, and she said she was reading about some people who died in a fire and it brought it all back to her when she had tried so hard to forget."

Her eyes suddenly widened and she sat back in her chair. Her hand went to her mouth. "Oh my goodness. I don't think I ever realized before, but that was the moment I knew that I wanted to help people be able to get past the bad things in their lives. Because my grandma was still crying over something that had happened long ago."

We sat in silence for several minutes. At last she took a deep breath. "Maybe we should trade chairs, Mrs. McGuire. You seem to be wearing the therapist's hat today."

"I bet she was so proud of you for making this your life's work."

"She was, she really was. She died about ten years ago. She was a hundred and three. An amazing woman."

"Wow."

"Long-lived genes in the family."

"Well, I knew it was unlikely that she could still be alive." I couldn't help a pang of disappointment, even as I scoffed at myself. She would be what, about a hundred and twelve? Be sensible.

"Actually, my dad talked about that explosion from time to time, even though Grandma didn't."

"He did?"

"Mm-hmm. He worked for Mr. Abernathy when he was in high school and college, during the summers. Grandma started at the plant during the war, World War Two. I think dad was about thirteen at the time."

"So he—he knew the family. Or at least knew about them."

"Oh, sure. It always sounded like a pretty close-knit group who worked there. Dad used to talk about the company picnic they had every summer, and the Christmas party. Not like office parties you hear about now, with everyone getting drunk and behaving inappropriately. Although no doubt that went on then, too, in some companies. But this was the whole staff from Mr. Abernathy who owned the business right on down to the janitor, and all their families, everyone dressed up in their best Sunday clothes. Dad used to tell me about how Mr. Abernathy asked him to be Santa Claus once when he was in college and how much fun it had been to hand out presents to all the kids who were there. I think he never forgot it because that turned out to be the very last time. The next Fall the explosion happened." She sighed and shook her head. "The last Christmas party. Sounds like the title of a thriller. I'm sorry, Mrs. McGuire, I'm going on and on. So what is your interest in that explosion?"

I pointed to the picture, which she still held. "The woman in that photo is Eloise Abernathy, and she died that night. But—"

"Wait a minute." She held up the picture and looked at it again. "Are you—how can you be the baby in this picture? They thought she was with her mother. I can't remember the baby's name, Lisa or—"

"Louisa. I don't know how it happened, but I'm becoming more and more certain this is a picture of me. I think I mentioned I still have the dress this baby is wearing, which is handmade and has a tag with my name in it."

"But everyone said the baby died."

"I know. But that's not all."

I pulled the article about the investigation into Frank Abernathy and the missing money out of my bag and handed it to her. "This is how I found your grandmother's name, and from her name to you." While she scanned it, I retrieved the obituaries and the family photo of my birthday, and handed them over as well.

She looked back and forth between them, then slowly raised her eyes to me.

"They...you..." She looked profoundly shocked.

"I know. I hope you believe me when I say I knew nothing of any of this until I just happened upon a picture of a woman who looked like me, holding a baby."

Several seconds ticked by, and at last she nodded. "I meet a lot of liars in this office. Some are lying to me, some are lying to themselves. But I get no sense of—of untruth from you."

"Thank you."

"And so how can I help? What are you trying to achieve?"

"I'm still figuring that out," I confessed. "I never had the slightest inkling that the woman in that picture, watching me blow out birthday candles, was not my mother. Even though—" I stopped, unable to continue.

"Even though?" she prompted gently.

"Even though, no matter what I did, I could never make her love me." A tear, unbidden and unwanted, rolled down my cheek. I reached for a tissue, and the act of pulling it through the nose of the ridiculous dispenser made me give a watery chuckle. "I see why you keep this guy here.

Dr. Wingate smiled. "Good, Fred has worked his absurdist magic once again."

"Anyway, she really, really loved my father, I knew that. But I was always closed out. And now I know why."

"Now you know why. And is that not enough?"

"I—I'm not sure yet. The thing is, I had an aunt, an aunt I never knew existed. If she's still alive, I'd like to find her."

"I see." She stopped, considered me, then rose and went to her desk. Opening the drawer, she pulled out a small pink phone and punched a couple of numbers. "Hang on," she said to me, "there's someone I'd like—" She broke off to listen, then spoke into the phone. "Hi, Dad, it's me...sure am, you?...Listen, there's someone I want you to meet. You'll like her. Her name is Louisa...okay, great. Yeah, let me check." She pulled the phone away from her face and said to me, "He's free tonight. Want to go see my dad?"

"Yes. Absolutely."

Returning to the little gadget, she said, "Tonight is good. I'll give her the address. Seven, right...Okay. Thanks!"

She pushed a button on the device and returned it to the drawer. She pulled out a piece of paper, scribbled several lines on it, folded it. Crossing back to the chairs, she held out the paper to me.

"Here you go. The next step in your quest."

Outside her building I squinted like an owl emerging into the light of day. Hoisting the straps of my bag over my shoulder, I turned left to walk to where I had parked my car. Behind me I heard several clicks accompanied by a whirring sound. I ignored it, thinking it was just some city noise, but it came again, and I realized I had heard these sounds before. I paused before a window in a men's clothing store, pretending to study the Italian pin-striped suit and silk shirt on display. Surreptitiously I slid my eyes to the side in time to catch movement by the recessed doorway I had passed moments before.

I have pretty good peripheral vision. And my hearing is just fine, thank you. That sound had been a motorized camera, snapping pictures at five frames every second. And the photographer who had dived into that doorway was Adler.

21

The only real sign that I was in a senior-living estate was the width and smoothness of the paths that crisscrossed the rolling campus. Otherwise I could have imagined myself in a primeval forest populated by elves. Or hobbits. Each separate little dwelling was different from its neighbors, each was adorably cute. Overhead, the evening breeze sighed through immense fir and redwood trees as the sun sank over the western hills.

I began to imagine Kay and me inhabiting a couple of these cottages in two or three decades. I gave us each a futuristic three-wheeled cart to drive on the wide, smooth paths as well as brightly-colored walking sticks with which to poke any whippersnappers who wouldn't get out of our way. Or maybe we could get a couple of those Segways and have races.

Of course we'd probably need to rob a couple of banks to be able to afford living here.

Then my footsteps slowed and stopped as I realized the image in my head of my future included my cousin, but Bob was not in the picture.

That doesn't mean anything, I reassured myself. It's just that I've known Kay longer. I gave my head a shake and walked on.

I had checked in at the gated entrance and been given a map with the Wingate cottage's location marked. After parking in the visitor area, I looked at the map in my hand and followed the fork in the path to the left. A few minutes later I arrived at Dr. Wingate's father's cottage, which had a neatly engraved brass plaque over the doorbell that read "Dr. Wingate."

Doctoring must run in the family.

I had barely pushed the bell when the door opened. The nonagenarian who stood there was so exactly my height that I almost felt required to say something about seeing eye-to-eye.

"Dr. Wingate? I'm Louisa McGuire. Your daughter—"

"So you are Eloise's baby Louisa, all grown up. I never thought I'd see this day. Come in, come in." He stepped back, holding the door open. A slight tremor animated his head, so that he seemed to be nodding agreeably at all times. Large round glasses rode low on his nose, and he was almost completely bald. The collar of his plaid Pendleton shirt was loose around his neck, giving the impression that he had shrunk. Or that he would be able to pull in his head like a turtle.

He closed the door behind me. "After my daughter called this afternoon I found I could think of nothing but what you might look like." He led the way to a pair of wooden rocking chairs in the living room. "And here you are and I would have known you anywhere. You look so much like your mother. Though I see something of your father in you too, especially around the eyes."

He carefully lowered himself into one of the chairs, and I sat in the other.

"I'm afraid I never knew anything about—about my family here. It was only by chance that I ran across this picture of my mother."

Once again I pulled the portrait of Eloise out of my bag and handed it to him. He smiled down at it, adding a bit of side to side shaking of his head to the tremor.

"A promising life, cut so, so short," he murmured. "Nineteen years old. Just a baby herself, really."

"It's so hard to think of someone dying that young."

"One knows it happens all the time, but when it's someone you know...And of course I'd known her for years. I think she was about eight when my mother went to work for her father. And her sister was just a toddler, maybe three."

"Your daughter said you and your mother both worked there."

"That's right. Mr. A gave me summer jobs in high school and college. I was in medical school by the time of the explosion, but I still saw them all at various gatherings. He asked me to play Santa Claus at the staff Christmas party. The last one."

He stared off into the middle distance, smiling. Perhaps handing out elaborately wrapped gifts in memory. If the explosion had not happened, I wondered if he would have played Santa to my toddler self.

I drew another picture from my bag. "Dr. Wingate, I'm wondering if you can tell me anything about this woman?"

He took the proffered photo, glanced at it, then gave it a longer look. "Ohhhh yes, her. Mr. A's private secretary. Let's see, was it Jane? Jan? No, Joan, that was her name. Efficient. Intelligent. Cold. My mother did not care for her."

"For any particular reason?"

He pursed his lips as he thought. "Well...of course this is simply gossip. Tittle-tattle I overheard my mother telling my father."

"Can't hurt anyone now," I encouraged.

"True. Well, when she first came to work for Mr. A, my mother was sure that Joan had designs on him. He was a good deal older than she, but very— prosperous. Joan's background—well, she never talked about her family or where she had come from. Mother always thought she'd grown up dirt poor. Mr. Abernathy would have been quite a catch. But if she was after him, he never was caught. Then later, I was pretty sure there was something between her and Carter Chessman. Your father. I think she may even have gotten him his first job there."

173

"That's interesting."

"I believe he started out as a salesman, but before long he was head of sales and Mr. A's fair-haired boy. And then—"

He broke off, and looked at me consideringly.

"Then what?"

"I suppose you're old enough not to be shocked by this."

"I—I'll try," I promised seriously. Really, after the revelations of the past few days, I felt I was beyond being surprised by anything.

"Well, there was the annual company picnic that June. Eloise and Leonora were there with their dad, and everyone who worked for the company and their families. Except for some reason Joan couldn't be there. There was certainly some drinking going on, and Eloise had just graduated from high school and was probably feeling her oats. My mother said that she and Carter disappeared for most of the afternoon. And the next thing we knew, they were engaged and then married and then the baby arrived. You. I think everyone suspected that the company picnic had a lot to do with Mr. A becoming a grandfather."

"Ah. Don't worry, I'm not shocked." Nor even a little surprised.

"I do remember Mother saying how snippy Joan was about it all. And when the staff chipped in for a wedding present, and then a baby gift, Joan refused to give even a dime. After the explosion, I remember Mother saying she was sorry about the things she'd said about Joan."

"Your mother sounds like she was a very nice woman."

He beamed at me. "She was. Really a lovely woman. I don't think she ever truly got over the tragedy. She felt things very deeply. And then she believed it was her fault that the police suspected that Leonora had something to do with it. Ridiculous."

"Why would she have thought that?"

"Well—" He stopped, seeming to consider how to continue. "Lennie—Leonora—had always...well, she seemed to know about things that hadn't happened yet."

I stared at him. "She was psychic?"

He shrugged. "Who knows for sure? Her father put it down to showing off and trying to get attention. And there's no question that she could be a little show off. My mother used to come home laughing about her antics, but I know that one time Mother answered the phone at the office—she was the receptionist—and it was Lennie, begging her not to go home at her usual time. The kid was so upset, she must have been about nine at the time, that Mother promised her she wouldn't, and being Mother, she felt she had to keep her word. And sure enough, just at the time she would normally have been driving down the hill from the plant, there was a good-sized earthquake and part of the road sheered away. No one was hurt, but if Mother had left at her usual time she might well have been killed."

"Wow. So—did Leonora say something about the explosion? Before it happened, I mean?"

175

He gave a little nod. "A few days before, Leonora came by the printing plant to catch a ride home with her dad, and while she was waiting for him she begged my mother to keep Eloise away from there. Mother couldn't help remembering that earthquake and promised she'd try. But Mr. Abernathy overheard and told Lennie to stop talking nonsense, that it was high time she got over her ridiculous premonitions."

Dr. Wingate and I both sighed. "If only—" I began, but couldn't go on. He nodded.

"If only. But somehow Mother let it slip to the police when they questioned her about the explosion that Leonora had been upset before it happened. I know she always regretted that."

"Do you know where she is now? Leonora?"

He shook his head. "I'm sorry, I don't. After I finished my medical training I took my wife and baby daughter to live in New Mexico for several years. We came back here after my father died, but by then Mr. Abernathy was gone and I had my career and family. I never heard anything of Lennie again."

San Francisco, Midcentury

The couple with the crying baby stood near the wall, a short distance from the entrance to the International Room. Passersby averted their eyes from the obvious row being enacted, hoping the child would not be on their flight. The woman, small, dark, well-dressed, hissed venomously at the tall blond man. He

176

held the child face out, jiggling it up and down in the crook of his arm, his expression blank, shut down.

A few feet away, just inside the entry to the famous bar, Emily Henderson glanced at the tiny watch on her wrist and hoped that her feet would hold out for the last forty minutes of her shift. She smiled at a man shrugging into his tweed topcoat as he exited past her, wishing him a safe flight. She did her best to tune out the argument going on outside the door, but it was impossible not to hear.

"I don't care. This is not what I signed up for. Forget it." The intensity of anger in the woman's voice was searing.

"Joan, please. What was I supposed to do?"

"Walk away. All you had to do was just—walk away."

The baby's cries grew quieter, sounding unutterably weary.

"I—I couldn't. I didn't even know what I was doing. One second my car blows up, the next thing I know I'm running down the hill with Louisa."

Emily's brows knit together in consternation. A car blew up? What was going on with those people?

The angry woman's voice became scaldingly cold. "You were an idiot to be there at all. Even so, you didn't have to bring it here."

"What? What are you talking about?"

"You should have ditched it somewhere. Someone would have heard it crying and found it." There was a pause, then in a more considering tone the woman said, "In fact, we still could."

177

Emily felt a chill drag across her shoulders. Her throbbing feet were forgotten. She took a quick step to the doorway and peeked out, in time to see the man stiffen. When he spoke, his low voice was almost as cold as the woman's.

"You listen to me, and you listen good. I've done a lot of things I'm not proud of, but one thing I am not capable of is abandoning a baby to die. *My* baby. So if you can't step up, you can just clear out now. And if you stay, we will never have this conversation again."

The baby's cries slowed to a hiccup, and she gave a big sigh. Tense silence teetered between the man and woman. The baby suddenly reached out and grabbed one of the large buttons on the front of the woman's suit. The button popped off. The baby put it in her mouth and smiled.

The woman took a step backward as though she had been struck. But she did not walk away.

22

When I returned to Bob's house after visiting Dr. Wingate, I was surprised at the number of cars parked on the street. Fortunately the cottage had a little detached garage and a driveway, so I didn't have to scout the neighborhood looking for a place to leave my car. Someone must be having a party, I thought.

I was even more surprised when I let myself in the front door to discover that the party was here.

Under a hubbub of voices I heard the Ellis Marsalis jazz CD I'd given Bob for his birthday. Debbie, whom I'd met at the other party, was seated on the sofa by Erik Landisen, conversing seriously and demonstrating the size of something with her hands. By the fireplace, two women who looked vaguely familiar were talking to the man who had popped into the Landisen's kitchen to order me to bring out more food. More people were in the dining room, standing by the table and noshing on something chippy and dippy there. Everyone held a wine glass or a bottle of beer. Neither Bob nor the dogs were in sight.

I closed the door behind me. Evidently my cloaking device was still activated, because no one even glanced my way. Did I know about this and just forget it was tonight? Hell no, I thought indignantly. I am not the kind of person who lets hosting a party slip from her brain.

"Louisa!" Bob's voice rose above the din as he emerged from the hallway that led to the bathroom and bedrooms. He hurried over to me. "You're back! Sorry about all this, it just sort of happened."

"Happened? How does—"

He leaned down to kiss me. "Erik's having some trouble with his marriage, and I was trying to cheer him up, and, well, somehow all these people are here. Let me put your bag in the bedroom. Are you hungry? Want something to drink?"

I shook my head. "Um, I'll put my stuff away and take a minute to regroup. Then I'll come help."

"Okay," he said cheerfully. "If you don't see me I'm probably in the kitchen."

He bounced away, pausing to say a few words to one or two people and gathering up empty beer bottles as he headed toward the back of the house. I watched him for a moment before turning to the bedroom.

I found the door closed. When I opened it, Emily Ann and Jack swarmed up to me. Stepping in, I closed the door behind me and went to sit on the bed. Both dogs jumped up beside me. Jack draped himself over my lap.

"So they shut you out of the party, huh? Don't worry, sweeties, you are not missing a thing." I gave Emily Ann a hug and massaged Jack's neck. "Do you think anyone would notice if I just stayed in here with you? Yeah, I don't think so either. Well, that Adler person might, but I'm pretty sure she's not here yet because she was following me again this evening. I saw her a couple of cars behind me at some stop lights. No doubt she'll show up as soon as she finds a parking spot. I'm kind of hungry though, I haven't had any dinner."

They both looked very interested when I said dinner.

"Hey, have you guys been fed?" Their expressions assured me they had not, but I'd been taken in before. "I'd better check with Bob. I don't think he could forget something that important. You wait here while I make sure you're not really starving to death. I'll come get you for a potty break soon. Believe me, you don't want to go out there. Someone might step on you. This group has raised not seeing large moving objects to an art form."

I stowed my purse and the canvas bag on a shelf in the closet and hung up my jacket. I looked down at myself and decided if I was dressed well enough for Dr. Wingate, I was fine for this group. Besides, I was invisible. I could probably wear the emperor's new clothes and get away with it.

"Wait here," I told the dogs, took a deep breath and pulled open the door.

181

"The dogs?" Bob looked up from the sofa, where I'd found him talking to Erik and Debbie. "I fed them in the bedroom when I got home. And then they were out in the yard for about twenty minutes."

"Good, thanks. They were claiming that they'd been forgotten."

Debbie giggled. "Your dogs can talk?"

"Of course." I figured she must never have lived with a dog.

"Louisa's dog Emily Ann is more the shy quiet type," Bob put in, "but my dog Jack is quite the conversationalist. Of course Louisa speaks dog fluently."

"I wonder if there's been any research done on this," Erik said. He fidgeted with the empty wine glass in his hand. "The—the human-canine bond and the development of two-way communication between the species."

He sounded gravely thoughtful and more than a little drunk. Bob sent me a private smile and a wink.

"We'll have to look that up. Sounds interesting. Can I get anyone anything? Debbie? Erik? Bob?"

"Welllll, if you're passing by a bottle, I'd love another glass of wine." Erik gave me an ingratiating smile.

"Oh, me too," Debbie said. "But let me—"

"No, stay where you are. I'll just be a minute."

I returned with a couple open bottles of wine and several glasses on a tray, and the dog leashes looped around my neck. Adler had arrived and settled herself on the floor by the sofa. She was patting Erik's thigh and giving him a soulfully sympathetic look.

"I am just so sorry to hear this. You and Maria—I never thought this would happen. How are you bearing up?"

He gave a deep sigh. "I—I'm doing all right. Really. Of course, I knew we had our problems, but I really thought—" He sighed again, then noticed my presence. "Oh, Lisa, thank you. Drowning my sorrows, I'm afraid." He gave me a brave, tremulous smile and held out his wine glass. I poured some wine into it, then set the bottle down.

"Will you all excuse me? I need to let the dogs out for a few minutes."

Bob surged to his feet. "No, let me, Louisa. You haven't even had a glass of wine yet. You sit here and I'll take them out."

He grabbed the leashes. Short of resorting to a spirited game of tug of war, I was trapped. I sat down on the sofa between Erik and Debbie. Bob poured a glass of wine and held out to me. I took it by the stem, and he hurried away.

I sipped some wine. Erik sipped some wine, and sighed. Debbie fiddled with her wineglass, then sipped. Our little group became a bubble of silence amid the waves of sound surrounding us. At Erik's feet, Adler reached out a languid arm to pick up a wineglass from the tray. She smiled at the three of us lined up on the sofa.

"Could someone pour? Please?"

Debbie hastily set down her glass and picked up the wine bottle. "Of course, sorry, I should have—"

She reached across me to pour, and managed to drip some of the dark red liquid onto my linen slacks. She didn't notice, but Adler did, and smiled. Debbie returned the wine bottle to the tray and turned to me.

"So how are you liking it here?" she asked brightly. "Are you having a good visit?"

"Yes, thanks, very good. This is such a great time of year to be in the Bay Area."

"I think Bob said you're thinking about moving here?"

"Mmm, thinking about it," I agreed, maintaining a meaningless smile.

"Actually, Louisa's been having a *very* interesting time." Adler's words were as smooth as cream. "She's just found out she comes from a family of swindlers and arsonists and has been quite busy looking them all up."

"What!" Debbie exclaimed, clearly not sure whether to laugh or not. She drew back to look at me, then at Adler. "Oh, she's joking. Adler, be serious for once."

On my other side, Erik stirred. "What's that, Adler? I'm afraid I was off in my own little world."

"It was nothing," Debbie told him, shaking her head and smiling at Adler.

"I am serious," Adler assured them.

I leaned forward. "And while I've been enjoying my visit here, Adler has been having fun herself by following me around and taking pictures."

184

Her eyes widened and she stared at me. I stood before she could say anything.

"Excuse me, please. I need some air."

Oakland, Midcentury

"I tell ya, that's the guy had me take him back up there." The cabbie pointed to the middle picture in the assortment on the desk.

Detective Olivetti pursed his lips and stared at the cabbie, who shrank in his chair. His short sleeved white shirt was wrinkled from a long day in his taxi, and what little hair he had looked as though it had been stirred with an egg whisk. Olivetti pulled a crumpled cigarette packet from the inside pocket of his suit jacket, pulled out a fag, put away the packet.

"How can you be so sure?" He picked up the lighter that lay on the desk blotter and flicked it. The cabbie looked hungrily at the smoke that rose when the cigarette was lit.

"He was in my cab a long time. We made a couple, three stops downtown, then we went to the guy's house."

"How do you know it was his house?"

"Well, uh, he just walked right in. He—he had a key. That's right. He had a key in his pocket and he unlocked the front door and went in."

"Coulda been his mother's house." Olivetti managed to blow smoke and sneer at the same time. "Did you hear him call out 'mom, mom, I'm home' when he went in?"

"No. 'Course not. He just went in. Told me to wait and went in. Then in a few minutes he came running out and told me to take him back to that printing place where I picked him up."

"Then what?"

"He kept saying faster, faster the whole way. We was almost all the way up the hill when there was this loud kaboom. You know? Like being back in the war. I thought maybe it was a earthquake, the way the ground shook."

"Earthquakes don't go kaboom."

"Yeah, so it wasn't an earthquake. That's just what I thought at the time. I didn't know, you know? So we come over the top of the hill and it was—it was—" He stopped, swallowing hard.

"It was what?" Olivetti prodded.

"Hey, man, can't you spare a smoke?"

Olivetti shrugged, fished out another cigarette, handed it over. He flicked the lighter. "It was what?"

The cabbie leaned forward to touch the cigarette to the flame and took a deep drag. His hand shook.

"It was hell, man, it was hell."

23

The padded chaise in the backyard under the stately oak tree was a lovely spot to linger with my steaming mug of tea. Birds went about their business overhead, squirrels scampered saucily along the highway of branches, and the morning breeze through the end-of-the-season leaves made a soothing rustle that masked the more urban sounds of people and traffic beyond the fence.

Occasionally a few acorns rained down on my head, but they weren't big enough to cause damage.

Emily Ann reposed in the grass to my right, long elegant legs crossed at the paws, while Jack had fallen over on his side to my left. I looked down at him, stretched out to the full, snoring ever so slightly. I could hardly bear the thought of leaving him behind.

But I didn't have to leave him behind. All I had to do was stay here.

Bob emerged from the back door, coffee mug in hand. He was freshly showered and dressed in a suit and tie, which reminded me that he had some sort of meeting this morning. Something about a funding board, reporting on the progress of the research project he was involved in. He looked dignified and responsible and intelligent, exactly the sort of person that funding boards would continue to fund. The sort of person any sane woman would be proud to be seen with.

"Good morning!" he called, rousing the dogs. Jack ran to him and he bent over to scratch the dog's butt. "Jack, my man! Is he the good boy then? Who's got the ears? Them big old Dumbo ears?"

Perhaps Jack would not be an asset to his presentation to the board. But I loved it when he showed his dog lover side.

Bob straightened and came toward me, settling onto the other chaise. He took a sip of coffee.

"Man, I thought I'd never get the last of them out the door last night," he sighed. "You were smart to go to bed. I finally used all the wine he'd drunk as an excuse to call Erik a cab. He really did not want to go home."

"So Maria actually left him?"

"Lock, stock and two smoking barrels." He shook his head. "He said she already had an apartment and had moved into it with half their furniture. He got home from the university to find her waiting at the door to hand him her keys. I've heard some rumors

188

that she has been having an affair, so I guess there must have been something to it."

"The house is his then, not theirs?"

He nodded. "He inherited it from a bachelor uncle or something. You'd have to be a multi-millionaire to buy something like that around here in today's market."

I thought of Mr. Gallagher turning down a million dollar offer for his little Craftsman house on a regular old residential street. It was hard to imagine what Erik Landisen's house in the hills was worth.

"Anyway," Bob went on, "I want to apologize again for last night. You must have thought you'd come to the wrong place when you walked in the door."

"I admit I was taken aback. I was hoping I hadn't forgotten we were expecting people."

He shook his head. "No, as I think I said, it just happened. Erik was moping around the office and I felt bad for him, so I said why don't you come over for a drink. I hadn't even noticed Debbie was there inputting some data, and somehow she thought I'd invited her as well. Then Erik saw Daniel and said we're going to Bob's house, you should come along, and it just snowballed."

I smiled. "Like the story about the golden goose."

He stared at me, puzzled. "Golden goose?"

"You don't remember it? It's a fairy tale. Someone is rewarded with a golden goose, I can't remember why, but anyway, real gold feathers. And this girl tries to pluck one of the feathers to steal it, and she instantly gets stuck to the goose. And then the next person sticks too, and the next, and off they go, everyone stuck to the goose." I paused, remembering being about five years old and turning the pages of a book in my lap. "The picture in my book was kind of cool," I finished lamely.

"Um, okay. So, from what you're saying, that would make me the goose?"

"I guess you had to be there. I'll see if I can find the picture sometime."

"I suppose it did sound like a bunch of geese, honking away."

"At least they sounded like happy geese. Angry geese are scary. And Erik did seem to need the company. Say, do you know if Maria took the cat?"

"Cat?" The jump from geese to cat had clearly left him behind.

"You know, the cat that I fell in love with at their party."

"Oh, that cat. You seriously liked it that much?"

I nodded. "Oh yeah. That cat and I made a connection." I could still feel her muscular, lithe little body curled around my neck.

"No one has said anything about the cat. But if there's a good moment, I'll ask."

"Thanks. I know it's crazy, but still." I hesitated, then decided I might as well take the plunge. "I need another favor from you?"

"Yeah?" He sipped some more coffee. "What's that?"

Go on, say it. I took a deep breath. "I would appreciate it if you could tell Adler to stop following me around with her camera and recorder."

"What!" Coffee sputtered out. He wiped at his lips with the back of the hand not holding the mug, then looked down to see if any coffee had spotted his shirt.

"For the past several days I've been seeing her sneaking around taking pictures. Of me. I'm pretty sure that the other piece of equipment glued to her body is a recorder. I'm tired of it."

He stared at me with his mouth open. "Louisa, you—I'm sorry, but that's just—"

"Just what?" Everything inside me went quite, quite still.

"I—I think you must be mistaken. I mean, why in the world would she do that?"

"That's a very good question." I let a few seconds pass. He didn't say anything. "Has she said anything to you? About me? Asked any questions?"

"No, not really. Well, she asked me where you're from. And she was a little curious about the picture you found, and the newspaper clippings. But anyone would be."

"I suppose so. But most people, curious or not, wouldn't start following me with a camera."

He set the coffee cup down on the grass. "Louisa, that's—well, I just can't see it."

"So you don't believe me?"

"Well, I mean—" He shifted uncomfortably. "Of course I believe you. I mean I believe you believe it. But even if you have seen her around, that doesn't mean she's following you. It's just a coincidence. In its way, Berkeley is something of a small town, and people's paths do cross."

"I see. And the camera? The recorder?"

"She's a photographer. She nearly always has a camera with her."

I let out the breath I hadn't known I was holding. A lot of tension flowed out with it. I looked at him for a long moment, then finally said. "Maybe you're right."

His brow smoothed. He looked as though I had given him a reprieve.

I leaned down to give Emily Ann a pat. "So what time is your meeting with the board today?"

"It's at ten." He couldn't hide the his relief that we had veered away from the insane and back to normality. "I'd better run. I have to go by the office first."

"Good luck with it."

"Thanks. I think they'll be more than satisfied with the report."

"Great."

"What about you, do you have plans?"

I nodded. "A few errands, dog park, you know."

He stood. "How about a nice dinner out this evening? I owe you for last night."

"Sure, that would be great. I'll see you tonight."

I lifted my face for his kiss, and he was gone.

I sat for a long time, thinking about Bob and our time together. We had met almost a year ago, at a time of turmoil in both our lives. My experience with my husband made me reluctant to even think of having another relationship. But Bob was so unlike Roger that they barely seemed like the same species. We had had such fun together, shared so much laughter. I appreciated his gentleness and courtesy. And our lovemaking had been a revelation.

But maybe it was true that relationships that begin in heightened situations rarely survive. Bob had come to California four months ago, asking me to come with him at the time, but giving me time to consider. We had talked on the phone regularly, and seen each other via Skype. Thinking back over that period, I realized that while I was always glad to talk to him, my life did not seem incomplete with him gone.

I loved my home, my friends, the life I had made for myself over the past year. And I loved Bob, I knew that I did...but not enough.

Tonight I would tell him I would be leaving for Willow Falls tomorrow.

Would it have tipped the scales the other way if he had believe me this morning, when I told him Adler was following me? Probably not, or at least not in the other direction. I realized I would still be looking for a reason to leave.

And that in itself was reason enough.

I don't know if I made a sound, maybe I sighed just then. Jack got up and lumbered over to me, laying his great head in my lap, the long, soft black ears spread like a velvet skirt over my knees. I leaned over and kissed him between his eyes, and my hand shook only a little as I stroked him.

The graves were on a hillside, shaded by a couple of redwoods so tall they brought skyscrapers to mind. I settled on the grass, which was due for a mowing and rippled a little in the breeze. Jack lay beside me in the grass, but Emily Ann remained standing, as though she were on guard. I leaned my head back against her shoulder and felt her breathe.

No one had looked twice at the dogs; apparently this large, historic cemetery in Oakland was a favorite destination for dog walkers, including an impressively tattooed young man holding the leashes of at least seven dogs. I had also passed young mothers with babies in strollers, hikers with backpacks, a photographer shooting candid shots of a young couple beside a fountain, and two teens on roller skates who were probably playing hooky from school. I knew from the cemetery's website that many famous people were buried here, and that docent-led tours were available.

I wondered if the docents knew that some of these headstones marked empty graves.

This was clearly a family plot, surrounded by an ornate little iron fence about eighteen inches high. A large double gravestone on the left marked the final resting place of my great grandparents, Rose Altman Abernathy and Arthur John Abernathy. She had died in 1949, he in 1922. A similar stone was engraved

Lois Lisle Abernathy   Frank Arthur Abernathy
1913 – 1942   1901 – 1961

The stone on the right was pure black marble, deeply incised with the names of three people.

Eloise Rosamunde Abernathy Chessman
August 6, 1937 – October 19, 1956

Robert Carter Chessman
November 8, 1928 - October 19, 1956

Louisa Diane Chessman
April 2, 1956 - October 19, 1956

Room remained for at least two more graves, but there were no more headstones. The autumn sunlight that filtered through the tree branches warmed me, as did the sturdy presence of the two dogs. Jack shifted a little, and thumped his strong tail. I stroked the soft black ears.

"Weird, huh," I murmured. "This is not what I expected when we started out from Willow Falls."

Emily Ann sank into a down position.

"Thanks for being with me, you guys. I—I'm okay, but it helps to have friends along. Not everybody gets to visit their own grave." My words were barely above a sigh, but they heard. I took a breath. "Jack, Emily Ann and I are leaving tomorrow, and you're going to stay here with Bob. You—you belong to him, and even though we love you, I know that he loves you too."

He looked into my face with those soulful Basset eyes, clearly worried.

"I'm sorry, sweetie, I didn't mean to upset you. I wish I could make you understand that I so much do not want to leave you, but I have to. I promised. I thought maybe I could stay here with you and Bob, but—but I can't. I can't."

Jack heaved a big sigh.

"I know, baby. You're going to miss us too. But you'll have Bob, and Daphne and Penny will be just up the street."

Emily Ann turned her head to look into my eyes.

"I thought I still had a decision to make. But this morning when he didn't believe me about that woman following us around—"

Jack sneezed. Or maybe it was a snort. As an editorial comment, it was perfect, and I laughed. The tears retreated.

"You said it, sweetie. You said it."

I put a hand on each of them and we sat quietly, gazing over the graves to the lovely view that stretched to the Bay. As I sat there, I realized what an intolerable weight had been lifted from me. I felt free, freer than I had in a long time. No more indecision about Bob. And no more guilt over a mother I had never been able to make a connection with.

I looked once more at the gravestone with its three names. Perhaps no one else in the world knew that all three names were false ones, presiding over an empty grave. Poor Eloise had perished in an eruption of fire and bedlam, and Carter Chessman had taken the baby and disappeared into the night. The Chessman family had ceased to exist as completely as if they all truly had been killed.

I thought of my childhood growing up with a mother who had resented and disliked me. I had never known why, and never been able to do anything about it.

"And now, thanks to you," I whispered to Jack, "I finally have the answer. It wasn't my fault at all. It was never my fault."

He thumped his tail twice. And I suddenly felt such a surge of happiness that I had to throw back my head and laugh, unable to contain the joy within me.

24

The wind sighing through the redwoods was not loud enough to cover up the sounds that came from behind and to my right. I didn't look around, but both dogs were alert to the presence there. They would ignore it as long as I did. We had all grown accustomed to the clicks and whirs from Adler's camera over the past few days.

I had had little expectation that calling her out on this behavior last night would have any effect. And here she was, clicking away, even in a cemetery. I truly had no idea what she was after. I'm hardly the stuff of reality shows, being one of the least photogenic people on earth.

I'm okay in person, I catch glimpses of myself in mirrors and plate glass windows and am never shocked or repelled by the sight. But the magic of photography turns me into someone who appears to have been let out on a weekend pass, either from a dementia ward or a minimum security prison, depending on what I'm wearing.

Knowing that she had to be getting truly terrible pictures was the only thing keeping me from turning the dogs loose. When I wasn't feeling enraged at the gall of the woman, I managed to see the humor in her having to look at a whole lot of awful pictures of me.

Served her right.

But now, sitting in this beautiful cemetery by the final resting place of relatives I hadn't known existed, the sound of that camera motor inexorably taking shot after shot brought back the feelings of rage with a vengeance. I would have loved to wreak some violence upon her. I thought with satisfaction of the time I had bitten an armed murderer and made him drop his weapon. Probably wouldn't get the chance to do that to Adler.

But I was prepared. And if all went well, maybe I'd even get to bite Adler before the day was over.

I pulled my phone out of my purse and dialed. "Hey, how's it going?" I kept my voice as low as possible. I've heard that a good directional mike can pick up conversations an amazing distance away. "Are you in place?...Okay, great, I'm ready to start. See you in a bit."

I dropped the phone into my pocket and climbed to my feet. I'm sure she got some extremely unflattering shots of my butt in the air, since I'm long past leaping to my feet. I slung my purse over my shoulder, made sure my grip on the leashes was secure, and set off

199

along the path, bidding a silent farewell to the Abernathy graves as I left them.

I roamed randomly, pausing to read headstones, gazing up at monuments and mausoleums. I kept my pace moderate, easy to follow, and follow she did. I didn't see her, but I heard the camera's motor frequently.

At last I came to the grove of trees I'd marked earlier, when I had studied the satellite view on Bob's computer. I put on a burst of speed and we race-walked out of the trees and around the corner of a mausoleum. I skidded to a stop, pressing myself against the back of the stone structure. I did my best to keep my panting silent as I caught my breath. And I waited. One hippopotamus, two hippopotamus, three hippopotamus, four—

She came flying around the corner of the mausoleum and swerved at the sight of me and the dogs. She teetered as she came to a stop. Before she could do anything—raise her camera, sneer a nasty comment—Penny too came around the corner, nearly bumping into her. And since she was expecting our tableau, she had her camera ready, and began shooting video of Adler.

Jack began to bark. I slackened the leashes, but didn't let go. Both dogs surged forward.

"What the—" Adler looked wildly back and forth between Penny and me. "What do you think you're doing? Keep those dogs away. You—"

"Now, that is exactly what I would like to know," I said. I gave a little tug on the leashes, and the dogs fell back a step. "What do you think you are doing?"

"I'm not doing anything. I'm just—"

Penny let go of the camera she was using, so that it swung from the strap around her neck. She grabbed another smaller model with a short lens, the one she had called a pancake lens. She stepped in close to Adler and started clicking away. Adler reared back, but Penny followed,

"What are you doing? Get away from me."

"Oh, man, Louisa, I can't wait for you to see these," Penny chortled, watching the video screen on the back of her camera. "Wait till we upload them on the University website. I'm talking viral."

Adler's expression went from petulant to alarmed. She flung out a hand to ward off Penny and her camera, and the long microphone in her hand nearly hit Penny in the eye.

"Hey, watch it. I can sue you for assault, and believe me, sister, with these shots I can make it stick."

Adler froze. Penny smiled.

"Look at that, Louisa. How much do you want to bet she's been sued before? Does she have any money? I wonder if she's insured. This just gets better and better."

Keeping a tight grip on the leashes, I moved forward, closing the gap between me and the other women. Penny also took a couple of steps. Adler's head swung left and right, her eyes jittering in their sockets as she looked for an escape. But the mausoleum blocked her way in one direction, and the dogs in the other.

"You're not going anywhere. At least not until I get some answers."

Adler glared at me, her upper lip held between her teeth. Perhaps to keep from showing her fangs. At last she snarled, "Well, what? What is it you want to know?"

I goggled at her. "Are you serious? What do you think? I want to know what's up with the cameras and the spying and following me around."

She stared back, equally incredulous. "What do you mean? You're a story. Of course I'm going to follow you around."

"I'm not a story. I'm a person minding my own business."

"You're a person who in the past year has been involved in at least four notorious news stories. And the minute you come to California, you just happen to learn that your real mother was killed when you were a baby and you were raised by an imposter who stole thousands of dollars from your grandfather's business. And *that*, my dear Louisa, is a story."

I ground my teeth together, thinking, Let's. Kill. Bob. That blabbermouth. Or maybe let's kill her, then Bob.

I shouldn't have hesitated. It gave her a chance to regroup.

"Here's something I've been dying to know," she said. She sounded like a mix between an ace reporter

202

and a sorority girl scoring the latest gossip. "Exactly where were you the night your husband died?"

That did it.

I started to laugh, and couldn't stop.

I laughed and laughed, gasping for breath. Both Adler and Penny stared at me, and the sight of their shocked faces made me laugh harder. I noticed some steps up to the main path a little way off and stumbled over to sit down. The dogs crowded close, sniffing my face and giving me little licks. Which made me laugh more.

It was several minutes before I regained a modicum of control. I tried to speak, but I kept wheezing.

"You want—to know—where I was the—" I had to stop again. A few deep breaths helped. I reached out to touch Emily Ann. "Oh, man. Okay. I'm okay. Maybe. Say, Penny, do something for me."

"Sure, anything." Anything to get you to stop laughing, her expression clearly stated.

"Make sure she's not still recording."

Adler turned bright red. Penny exclaimed, "You bitch. Give me that bag."

She grabbed the equipment bag off Adler's shoulder and tore it open, poking around inside. At last she drew out something small encased in black plastic.

"I think this is it."

"No, stop—"

I watched Adler's face. "That's a decoy," I said. "What's that thing hanging around her neck?"

This time the chagrin was much more real.

"I thought it was a light meter," Penny confessed. She removed it from Adler's neck and poked at buttons until a little green light went off.

"To answer your question, Adler, I was home with my dog. I was certainly not in a certain downtown Seattle restaurant with Roger and his bimbo lawyerette."

Penny looked confused. "Why is she asking about your husband?"

"Because he died in the stupidest way possible. You probably heard about it. The idiot lawyer whose companion was under the table giving him a blow job while he choked on a piece of steak. She thought he was enjoying her—ministrations, when what he really needed was the Heimlich maneuver."

"Oh my god, that was your husband?"

I sighed. "Told you you'd heard about it."

"Well, I really only paid attention because of the fire angle."

"Fire?"

"Yeah, don't you remember? When he slumped forward he knocked over the candle on the table and set the tablecloth on fire. There was so much confusion with the woman coming out from under the table and the guy, your husband I mean, being, well, dead, that the fire nearly got out of control. Several tables caught fire."

"You see!" Adler looked very pleased. "Total chaos and confusion. She could easily have been there and slipped away."

I was capable only of staring at her open-mouthed. Penny however rounded on her angrily.

"Don't be an idiot. Of course she wasn't there. That's the stupidest thing I ever heard of."

"Even though she had just kicked him out of their home, and was planning to divorce him? We all know who comes out ahead when a housewife divorces an attorney."

"I wasn't—" I began, and stopped. What did it matter if I was or wasn't a housewife, or planning to divorce him for that matter. I shook my head. "Did not kill husband, period. Anything else you want cleared up for your exposé?"

"It's just odd how trouble follows you around, and you always come out better for it. You put a respected banker in prison, and suddenly your cousin's antique business is booming."

"Mmmhmm. Of course that was after the banker had murdered at least two people, shot his sister-in-law, and planned to murder Bob. Anything else?"

"That poor woman who tried to get herself out of a financial hole with a few counterfeit traveler's checks—"

"Right, the one who was into the mob for many, many thousands of dollars in gambling debts. The one who tried to shoot me. At least you're only trying to shoot me with a camera. Makes a nice change."

"And it's only been a few weeks ago that a respected British peer was drawn into one of your schemes with—"

"Yeah, yeah, the fabled golden frog of Ramses the Fourth. Or whatever the heck they were calling it." I stared at her long enough for her to begin to fidget. "You know what your problem is, Adler?"

"Aside from being a bitch," Penny threw in. I nodded.

"Aside from that. Your problem is that you actually believe the bullshit that your, um, let's call them colleagues, come up with. It doesn't matter what actually happens or to whom or how it affects them. There's a twenty-four-seven news cycle to fill up, and the more lurid you can make it, the more hits you'll get on YouTube."

"I am a reputable photo journalist—" she began indignantly, but I interrupted in a bored tone.

"Yeah, yeah, sure you are. That phrase is getting to sound more and more like an oxymoron, but whatever. I think in your case we can probably skip the claim of reputable."

I stood up from the steps. The dogs followed me back to Adler and Penny. "You know, if you hadn't decided to go fishing for me, you might have looked around and noticed who Penny is."

Adler glanced at the tall woman, then back to me. "What are you talking about?"

"You thought she was just Bob's neighbor, didn't you? Another woman with a dog, someone that a person with my—how do you suppose she would have phrased it to herself, Penny? Limited intelligence?"

Penny grinned. "I bet she did. Because women with dogs can't be very smart, can they?"

Adler's expression assured me we had pegged it.

"Yeah, I think that's it. She could just tell that you're probably a housewife—and I mean no disrespect to housewives—with a cute little dog, and not someone that a photo journalist should concern herself with." The words "photo journalist" came out with a satisfyingly sarcastic tone.

"When in reality, behind my apron and dust mop—" Penny could not contain her glee.

"Behind your apron and dust mop, you and that cute little dog are licensed detectives, respected arson investigators, and members of the famous Marquette Detective Agency, a Bay Area institution since the nineteen fifties."

"And by golly, does it pay off to have a detective agency at my disposal. As well as my dust mop. Because we found all kinds of good things about you, *Adler*." She snorted as she said the name. "Or would you rather be called Annette? Or Amy? Or how about Amanda Heather Mitchell? I think that one has quite a ring."

"All right, all right, so I changed my name. Big deal."

"As you say, no big deal. Usually. Kind of depends on the reason, and I have to admit, your reasons were pretty compelling. I wouldn't have wanted to go to jail either."

"I don't know, Penny, wouldn't you think a photo journalist would be eager to document the gritty underbelly of what goes on in a women's prison?"

She nodded. "Could be pretty compelling stuff, especially compared to anything she could make up about you. I think she missed out on a real opportunity. But maybe she'll have another chance, at least if she keeps on like she has been."

"Penny's become a really good friend," I said, reaching out and giving her arm a squeeze. "I know I can count on her to keep an eye on things here." I looked Adler full in the face. "On you."

Penny nodded. "Anything for a friend. So you run along now, Adler Amy Annette Amanda. If you want to think that you're a photo journalist, fine, but make sure that you're dotting all your T's and crossing all your I's. Because if you don't, I'm going to know, and so will everyone else. And Adler—"

Adler had already started moving, but she paused and looked back.

"—get rid of all those photos of Louisa. And I do mean *all*. She takes the worst pictures of anyone I've ever known."

25

Penny and I hugged for a long time on the sidewalk outside the café. When we stepped back, we both had tears in our eyes and smiles on our faces. She bent down and picked up Daphne.

"God, I'm going to miss you guys." She pulled a tissue from her pocket and gave a great honking blow of her nose. "See, I came prepared. I knew I was going to get emotional."

"Me too." I pulled out my own tissue. "But this is just goodbye for now, right? You're going to come and visit?"

"You bet. After that conference in Atlanta next month for sure. And of course I never know when we'll get called to a fire investigation in your neck of the woods, so we could be popping up any old time."

"Great. I can't wait."

"*I* can't wait to meet Kay, and go to your dog park, and see your octagonal house. My gosh, do you have any idea what your house would be worth if it were here?"

I laughed. "Yes I do, since everyone talks about real estate prices all the time. And it would be way more than I could afford."

We stood there, forcing passersby to go around us, giving each other goofy smiles. At last she heaved a big sigh.

"All right, I'm off. I hate to be late for client meetings."

"You can always blame the traffic."

"I'll just tell them that Daphne was driving and it's hard for her to reach the pedals."

She gave me one more quick, hard hug, gave Jack and Emily Ann each a quick pat, and turned to stride to her car. I watched until she turned out of sight around the corner, then looked down at my companions.

"I know we need to go home—" The word stuck in my throat. I took a breath. "—go back to Bob's house and pack, but let's walk up this street one more time. Maybe Nate Gallagher will have some new pictures in the window."

Penny and I had lunched at Mintie's, sitting at the same table on the patio that we had occupied on my first day. Ashley waited on us again, and had greeted me as warmly as she did Penny. As I looked over the day's menu, I had a little pang of regret that I would never get to eat my way through their entire repertoire. But there was always something new at the Bluebird Café, too.

210

"I found something else when I was looking for the dirt on Adler," Penny had said, selecting a whole wheat roll from the bread basket on the table. She broke off a piece and dabbed butter on it. "But I'm not sure—I don't know if you really want to hear about it."

"Go ahead. I've had a lot of practice lately hearing about stuff I didn't want to." I sipped some water, feeling more nervous than I wanted to appear.

"Well, there was a file in our archives from the explosion. The one that killed—killed Eloise."

"You mean your agency actually investigated it?"

She nodded. "It was such a big deal, I don't think anyone in the business wasn't involved. From the paperwork I saw, we weren't the main investigators. But some of what I read got me to thinking about the explosion itself. I have an idea about it."

"Tell me."

"Well, have you ever heard of the Texas City Disaster?"

I shook my head.

"It happened in 1947. Almost six hundred people were killed. I think it still holds the record for the deadliest industrial accident in U.S. history. They were loading ammonium nitrate onto a French ship—"

"Isn't that the stuff they used in Oklahoma City?"

She nodded. "The government used it in World War Two to make bombs. After the war I guess there was still a lot of it available, so they started selling it for fertilizer."

I shuddered. "That is just creepy, the idea of using the leftovers from bombs to grow stuff we eat."

211

"Yeah. Well, anyway, back then it wasn't regulated, pretty much anyone could get hold of it. The thing that happened in Texas City was so huge that it made the news everywhere. There were tons and tons of ammonium nitrate packed into the ship, and it caught fire. The captain didn't want to ruin the cargo by putting out the fire with water, so he ordered all the hatches closed and they piped in steam below decks to try to put it out, which didn't work. When it blew, the entire metal ship exploded. It knocked planes out of the sky. Wiped out a huge number of houses. I read somewhere that all of the water was blasted out of the port."

I gaped at her. "That's just—just—"

She nodded. "I know. The thing is, it was so widely reported that it's very possible that Joan and your—and Carter knew about it. We know your dad was in the army, he might have learned something about explosives there. And lots of women worked in munitions plants during the war. Plus, we don't know anything about Joan's background. Maybe her dad worked in mining or construction. Or even farming, since this stuff was used for fertilizer."

"So there was virtually no chance the printing plant explosion was an accident."

It wasn't a question.

She shook her head. "No. One or both of them did it deliberately. They may well not have known how big an explosion it would be, but they did do it. The only other possibility I can think of is that someone else, another employee, planted the stuff and managed to implicate them, but given what we know about their lives after the explosion it's pretty hard to go there. I'm sorry."

"I can't believe that Eloise being there was anything other than an accident though."

"Oh, me neither. Absolutely."

"I realized something earlier, when I was at their graves."

"That must have been hard. I mean, seeing your own name—"

I shook my head. "Oddly enough, it wasn't. Probably because I know those graves are empty. It was actually pretty peaceful. But what I realized was, finding out that Joan was not my mother is the best thing that's ever happened to me. I know that that I— I did have a mother who loved me. I don't mean to be ungrateful for anything Joan did do for me, but—all I can say is, I truly feel like a new person. And really happy."

Now, walking up the street with Emily Ann and Jack, my steps felt light. I finally let Emily Ann lead the way into the pet store, where we bought locally made treats for some of our special dog friends. We window shopped the toy store, and I resisted the urge to go into the midcentury store. The chance of my drooling onto some high end upholstery seemed too great. And I wasn't sure how they would feel about a greyhound on one of their sofas. Emily Ann can never resist a sofa.

We came to the last storefront before the photography studio. The Inward Horizon. I liked the name, and wondered idly what sort of life reading Madame Nora would give me. I paused to see what was on display in the window. Before I could focus on the books and other items there, Jack dragged me toward the Dutch door. Both halves were open today. In a moment he was inside the shop, Emily Ann right behind him.

They have very good leash manners and pull so seldom that I was unprepared, and could only follow.

The light inside was dim after the dazzling sunshine on the street. I blinked, trying to make out my surroundings. A woman's voice spoke from the back of the shop.

"Come in, my darlings, come in. I've been waiting for you."

Again, both dogs strained on their leashes to reach her. She came out from behind a glass-fronted counter and knelt down, gathering both dogs into a hug. They snuffled and wagged in ecstasy, and Jack even uttered the little high pitched cries he makes when he is reunited with a favorite person.

"There you are," the woman said, burying her face in Emily Ann's neck. "Yes, sweeties, yes, oh yes, you are the good, good dogs. You have taken such good care of our Louisa."

I watched in confusion. I had no idea who she was, but both dogs acted as though she was someone they knew well and loved. From what I could see of her she was older, perhaps mid-seventies, though she moved with a lithe grace I could only envy. Her thick gray hair was very long, nearly to the waist, flowing in ripples down her back and over her shoulders. She was dressed in a deep blue-green tunic of some supple fabric over close-cut dark blue pants. A bracelet of blue and green glass cubes circled her wrist. Her feet were bare.

At last she looked up at me and smiled, rising easily back to her feet. I stared at her, puzzled. I was sure somehow that I knew her, but had no context in which to place her. I noticed a smattering of freckles decorating her clear un-made-up face, delicately arched brows, and very blue eyes.

"So, Louisa, here you are at last."

And then I knew. Leonora. Lennie.

Madame Nora.

I burst into tears.

Willow Falls, October 19, 1961

Louisa let herself in the kitchen door and listened carefully. The house was quiet; no hint of where her mother might be. It had been a pretty good day in kindergarten, and Louisa didn't want to ruin it by making her mother mad.

Kindergarten was only half a day. It was noon and Louisa was hungry. The milk they had drunk at school midmorning was no substitute for lunch. But Louisa was used to making her own lunch. She walked quietly to the refrigerator and found an apple and some slices of cheese. She put them on the table, then fetched the glass jar of mayonnaise. She carefully spread some on one slice of Wonder Bread, added one slice of cheese, and folded it to make a sandwich. Before she took a bite, she put the rest of the cheese, the mayonnaise, and the bread away.

Since no one was in the kitchen to tell her not to, she alternated bites of her sandwich and her apple. She hummed a little tune to herself as she ate, enjoying having both lunch and dessert at the same time. Her mother would have made her eat all of the sandwich before she touched the apple.

Kindergarten had a lot of rules too, but Louisa liked going anyway. Mrs. Platt was her teacher, and she was calm and fair. They were learning about time and dates now, and Mrs. Platt had showed them something really neat that morning.

"Look, class," she had said, writing four numbers on a piece of paper in her large clear hand, "this is a very special year. Look at the numbers, nineteen sixty one. Now we turn it over and—oh my goodness, it's the same upside down!"

Louisa had gaped. It *was* the same! Somehow it seemed like magic. Of course, Mrs. Platt had written a curvy nine like in a book instead of a balloon on a stick nine like she was used to writing, but still.

"This is the only year in your whole life that the year will be the same upside down," Mrs. Platt had continued. "Isn't that wonderful?"

Louisa finished her lunch and made sure there were no crumbs on the table. She wanted to find some paper and a pencil or crayon so she could practice making curvy nines. She was going to show Kay the upside-down-year trick. She loved being able to show off what she learned in kindergarten. Kay was still mad that she had to wait until next year to go to school.

She left the kitchen and quietly walked through the dining room. Daddy might have some paper in his den. The house was completely still; her mother must be out.

The door to the den was open and she stepped through, stopping short when she saw her father. He was sitting in his easy chair, staring out the window. There was a crystal tumbler near his hand on the table beside the chair. Louisa saw that it was nearly full of that brown stuff her parents liked to drink. Louisa had tasted it once and spit it out. It was awful. People must change a lot when they grew up to be able to drink something that tasted that bad.

She hoped this was the first glassful. If it was everything should be okay. If he had already drunk a glass, maybe not. She started to tiptoe away, but he noticed her in the doorway.

"Oh, Louisa, are you home already?"

She relaxed. He sounded okay. But his face looked sad. She took a few steps closer.

"Your mother went shopping."

Louisa nodded. Her mother always went shopping. She took a deep breath. "Daddy, can I have a piece of paper? I want to practice numbers."

"Sure. Take all you want. It's in the middle drawer in the desk."

She found the paper and daringly took three sheets. She turned to go, but stopped when she saw his expression. He was staring out the window, and the early afternoon light fell across his face. Was he— was he *crying*? Louisa felt shocked to her bones. Daddies did not cry.

"Daddy, are you all right?"

He pressed his lips together and swiped at his face with the back of his hand. When he looked at her, she saw he was trying to smile. "Sure, I'm okay. I was just thinking." He paused, and his gaze went to the window again. "It's only—oh god, Louisa, why couldn't your mother have just done what I told her?"

He fell silent again, and after a while Louisa tiptoed away.

26

Bob was beaming when he came home that evening. "Honey, I'm home!" he called in a retro TV sitcom sing-song.

I was sitting on the sofa just a few feet from the front door. "Honey, I'm right here."

He dropped his briefcase and came to sit beside me. Jack jumped up on his other side, his heavy tail thumping a syncopated rhythm against the back of the sofa. "Jack, my man! Catch any squirrels today?"

I bit my lip to keep from saying, no, but he helped catch a rat. Instead, I leaned over and kissed his cheek, realizing it could be the last time I would do this. I suddenly wanted to cry, but managed to keep my voice steady.

"Your meeting must have gone well."

"Sure did. The board got really excited about one of the new projects we proposed."

"That's great. What project?"

"The one Adler came up with, showing how medical hypnosis is being used all over the world. It could lead to forming an international task force to train new practitioners in places where hospitals are scarce."

Another Adler plan.

"How excited did the board get? Did they actually come up with the funding, or they just liked the idea?"

He picked up one of Jack's ears and let it drop. "Funding for the first six months, renewable for another two years if they like what we've done at that point."

"That's wonderful. Really huge. Congratulations."

He reached for my hand. "Of course it means lots of travel."

I took a deep breath. I had spent all afternoon rehearsing ways to get into this conversation. I tried to keep my tone light. "Speaking of travel, I'm doing some too."

His hold on my hand tightened, and his smile disappeared as he searched my face. "What do you mean?"

"I've decided to go home tomorrow."

I could practically hear the words fall to the floor with a thud. The sound of a car grinding its gears as it passed down the street filled the silence between us. Then Jack rose to his feet, placed his short front legs in Bob's lap, and stretched out his neck to plant a puppy smooch on my arm. I reached over with my free hand and rubbed his nose.

At last Bob spoke. His tone was even. "I really screwed up this morning, didn't I?"

Years of habit, of always taking any blame upon myself, nearly made me deny it. I had learned very young to avoid confrontations. Most of my life I had taken refuge in silence. But this time I could not take the silent path.

"This morning didn't help," I acknowledged, "but that's not really it. Or not all of it. I just—I'm ready to go back to my own life."

"And you can't see yourself having a life with me?"

"I've been trying. But when I picture the future, I keep seeing me in my house in Willow Falls, and I'm so sorry, but you aren't there."

He bit his lower lip, but said nothing.

"Our time together has been, well, I don't even have the words. You may not know it, but you've given me—oh, so much. A sense of self. I have no idea who or what I would have been if we hadn't met."

"You'd probably still be trying to break into strangers' cars," he said, referring to our first encounter. I'd been trying to unlock what I thought was my car, but was actually his.

I felt a rush of relief. He wasn't going to yell at me. Or worse. This was Bob, not my horrible husband Roger. I could say whatever I needed to say.

"True. I still can't believe I didn't notice there was no Emily Ann in that car."

"Maybe the hand of fate had something to do with it."

"Or the blindfold of fate. I mean, my own car was only about fifteen feet away."

"If you hadn't tried to steal my car, I would most likely be dead. Anything I accomplish for the rest of my life I owe to you."

Tears sprang to my eyes. "Bob, I—I wish I could stay, but—"

"But you can't." He exhaled a long breath, and looked away. "I feel like a damned fool for the way I've acted since you got here. I should have dropped everything the minute you arrived. I have no idea why I didn't. Self-importance, maybe."

"No! Stop it. If we were ever going to consider my moving here, I had to see what the life would be like. To be honest, I've realized what I really want is less attention, not more."

"Ouch."

"Oh, stop it." I gave his leg a little push. "You're going to be much happier being able to concentrate on your work and you know it. Jack will be as much responsibility as you need."

He shook his head. "I'm not at all sure I will be happier. But I truly do want what's best for you."

His tenderness made me catch my breath. "I know. As I do for you."

"Louisa, tell me, how much do you think finding out about your parents has affected you? Could you be reluctant to stay here because of what happened to your real mother? Because if that's the case—"

"No." The finality in my voice stopped him. "It's not that at all. I mean, of course I've been affected by

222

what I learned. But probably not in the way you're thinking. I feel..." I took a deep breath and felt it flow out again. "I feel freer than I have my whole life. I can't tell you the weight that's gone, realizing that my lack of connection with the woman I thought was my mother was never my fault. It's almost like I've been plunged back into adolescence and am on that roller coaster of figuring out who I am."

"I see."

"I really have no idea who I'll be when I grow up—again—but I think there's going to be a big streak of independence."

He gave me a grin. "Um, Louisa, that streak was already there."

"Well, it's going to be bigger. And probably louder. I suspect I'm going to become quite obnoxious."

He laughed and shook his head. But the word 'obnoxious' brought me back to the other topic I needed to broach. Once again I took a deep breath.

"There's something else." I had debated with myself about this for hours.

"What?"

"Come into your office. I need to use your computer."

I led the way, Bob and both dogs following. I pushed Bob into his chair and pulled over the stray dining chair he kept in the corner. Sitting, I said, "I wasn't sure whether to show you this. But—well, you're clearly going to be working closely with Adler. You should know what you're dealing with."

The computer had gone to sleep, but sprang to life when I reached past him and touched the mouse. I clicked on an icon. A skewed picture of trees and a path filled the screen. Another click and the video spring to life.

The image quality was jumpy because Penny had filmed as she ran after Adler. Bob stared at the screen on which the dogs and I hurried around a corner of a mausoleum. When Adler broke into a run to follow us he leaned forward, frowning. In a moment we were seeing my confrontation with Adler. The sound track was excellent. Penny had borrowed equipment from her agency to edit the video, and she clearly knew how to use it.

The scene played out. As it drew to a close, Bob fell back in his chair, shaking his head.

"I—I can't believe it. She—Louisa, I am so, well, embarrassed that I doubted what you told me this morning."

I clicked the pause button. The frame that filled the screen was of Adler's face, her eyes squinted and mouth pursed.

I was inordinately pleased that she did not look at all pretty.

"I know you like her, that you've enjoyed working with her. And that this new project you're starting will involve her."

"But how can it? I mean, once people know what she's done…"

"That's up to you. As long as she behaves herself, neither Penny nor I have any intention of sharing this.

But you need to know in order to protect yourself. She may be talented, but Bob, please do not trust her an inch."

"I'm going to have to think about all this. How can I go into this new project, working with someone I know I can't trust?"

"This is why I wasn't sure I should show you the video."

"No, you were right to show me. I need to work from knowledge, not ignorance."

"How vital is she to the project? I mean, it's not like there aren't other documentary filmmakers around."

"True. But it was her idea."

"Was it?" My distrust of the woman made me doubt anything I heard about her.

"Yes. Well, I mean, we've all been discussing possible strategies to expand the current work." He stared blankly at the computer screen. "Now that I think about it, it was Debbie who first said something about taking it global." His eyes widened in realization. "Oh my god, it was Debbie. And then somehow it became Adler's idea."

Bob turned to look at me. "I've got a lot to think about."

"I know. Just don't forget to feed your dog while you're doing all that thinking. And now, I don't know about you but I'm starving. Let's take the dogs and walk down to Mintie's."

He stood, then held out his hand to me. I took it, and he pulled me to my feet. "I feel like the condemned man eating a hearty last meal."

"Let reminisce about the happy times and not think about tomorrow. Okay?"

"Okay. We'll have plenty of time for dessert. I can think of a lot of happy times."

27

The car was nearly loaded. My clothes were in a couple of canvas bags, stuffed into the space behind the front seats. The Rubbermaid tote with dog food and supplies was in the back next to the windows. A stack of CDs rested between the seats, and a cooler with munchies was on the floor on the passenger side. Penny had stopped by earlier with a bag of goodies from Katrina's bakery; those were on top of the CDs, in easy reach.

"And *this* bag is for Bob," she said, handing it over to him. "Louisa, do not share yours with him. He can go down and get his own Danish any time he wants to."

He had laughed and promised not to invade my sacred bag. "It will be good to have something to motivate me to get up in the mornings," he told her.

She grabbed me for one more hug, then resolutely pushed me away. "All right, I'm leaving before I burst into unseemly tears. Call. Text. Email."

"I will, I will. You'll be sick of me." I hugged her back. "Now go."

I peered into the car, trying to think of anything I might have forgotten. Water. I had put a couple of partially filled bottles into the freezer last night. I closed up the car and locked it and followed Bob into the house. Emily Ann and Jack were waiting by the door. Packing the car had them on tenterhooks, waiting to see what would happen next. I led everyone to the kitchen.

"Nearly forgot these," I said, pulling the bottles out of the freezer.

"Here, let me." He took them and filled them from the big jug of water in the fridge. I found the canvas bag I'd hung in the pantry for them and he slid them inside.

"Thanks," I said.

"No problem," he replied, and surreptitiously looked at his watch. It was at least the third time I had noticed him check the time.

"Do you have an appointment or something? You don't have to wait. I can just take off when I'm ready."

"No! I mean, no, nothing like that. I just, well, okay, I'm expecting a delivery. For you. I thought it would be here by now."

I didn't know what to say. "Oh. Okay, thanks. Actually, it doesn't matter when I set off."

He looked at his watch again. "Honestly, you'll do better if you wait a bit. The worst traffic will be coming into the city and you'll be going the other way, but it will still be a bear."

"It does seem like you're better off here without a car, but I'm still sorry about drowning yours."

He gave me the first genuine smile of the morning. "I know. Isn't the traffic awful? And don't you just crack up every time someone talks about it?"

"My favorite is the way people always ask if you found a parking place. I mean, it's sort of a given. If you're not in your car then you must have somehow found a parking place."

"Try not to feel too smug when you get home to the land of acres of parking."

"I'll try," I assured him. "But I can't make any promises not to feel smug about real estate prices."

"Oh, god, I know," he groaned. "It's just absurd. And yet..."

"I know, it really is a great place. The weather, the energy, the food. I—I am so glad you've found work that you love here. And people who really seem to value you."

I set down the bag of water bottles and walked into his arms. He held me in a rocking hug for a long time.

"I'm going to miss you so much," he mumbled into my hair.

"I know. But—it's the right thing."

I felt him nod. "You're right. I know you're right."

The doorbell rang. Jack hurried into the living room, barking. Emily Ann stayed by my side; she was taking no chances. Bob's arms tightened for a moment, then he let me go. I picked up the bag and followed him to the front door. When he opened it, I was surprised to see Debbie on the porch.

"Hey, Debbie, come in," Bob said, holding the door wide. He leaned over to hold Jack's collar, then told him to sit.

"Hi, Debbie." I peered past Bob to greet her.

"Hey Louisa, Bob. I can't stay, I've got a class. Come on out to my car."

Bob turned to me and grabbed my hand. "Come wait here on the porch," he commanded, pulling me out of the house and closing the door on the dogs. Dropping my hand he started down the steps, then paused and looked back. "And close your eyes."

"Um, sure." I obeyed, listening to the morning sounds of the city. From up the street I heard a couple of barks that sounded suspiciously like Daphne. Bob and Debbie held a whispered consultation over something, then a car door closed. His steps sounded on the path and then the steps.

"Okay, open your eyes."

"Bob, you did it! Oh my gosh!"

I stepped forward to take Grizelda, the red Abyssinian cat from his arms. She tucked her head under my chin and turned on a purr that could power a Mac truck.

"Oh, sweetie! You're here!" I gave her a kiss on top of her sleek head, then looked up at Bob. "Thank you. I really, really—well, thank you."

He shook his head. "I couldn't believe it. I got to the office yesterday and Erik was there, and the first thing he said to me was did I know anyone who needed a cat."

"I knew she was supposed to be mine."

"And you were right. Not only that, he told me she actually likes to travel. They took her on a road trip last year and she loved it. She even has her own super fancy traveling crate. Look."

He pointed toward Debbie's car, where she was unloading cat equipment. Food and water bowls, a bag of food, a bag of litter. And a traveling crate with a cushion inside and even a little wired-in litter pan.

"Will it fit on the front seat of my car?" I asked, carrying my vibrating ball of warmth to the driveway. Bob picked up the crate and slid it in.

"Wow, looks like it was custom made," Debbie said. "Listen, I've got to run. Louisa, it was so nice getting to know you. Have a wonderful trip."

I shifted the cat so I could shake her hand. "You too, Debbie. Good luck with the research project and the degree."

With a wave she was gone. I took a deep breath.

"Guess I better get on the road."

He nodded, and gathered up the rest of the cat supplies. "Let me go find a bag for this stuff. I'll be back in a minute."

"Bob, thank you. For everything. Everything."

"Louisa, can I—can I call you?"

"I—I don't think we should. I'm sorry."

He nodded. "You're right." He stood for a moment looking at me. "Okay, be right back. Want me to bring Emily Ann out?"

"Yes, please, and I'll settle Miss Kitty in her condo."

I watched him go into the house, then turned to the car. The cat was perfectly willing to slide through the hatch on top of the crate and sat down on the cushion, her head sticking out the hatch. She gave me a slit-eyed smile.

"I am so happy to see you again," I told her. "And guess what? I was talking to my aunt yesterday—" I had to pause and swallow, feeling again the enormity of being able to say that. "Anyway, my Aunt Lennie, she knows things. And she told me you hate the name Grizelda."

"Mewp."

"Yeah, me too. And she said that you would rather be called Bliss."

"Prrrt!"

"Soon you'll meet your new sister Emily Ann, and then we're going to drive a long way. And then we'll be home."

"Mrrrp."

I heard the door to the house close behind me. "Okay, here we go, off to our new life."

I turned to see Bob approaching, yet another canvas bag in one hand, and both dogs' leashes in the other. He went to the back of the car and opened the hatch. Jack and Emily Ann jumped in. I bit my lip.

"I—I already said good bye to Jack," I said. I clenched my teeth hard. I didn't see how I could go through it again.

"He's coming with you."

"But—he's yours."

"He was my dog for a while. But he would be lost without you and Emily Ann. He is your dog. You have his heart." He reached up and closed the hatch. "Now go. Drive safely. Have a good trip." He blinked several times. "Have a good life."

I nodded, and got in the car, and drove away. In the rear view mirror I watched him, standing in the middle of the street watching me, until I turned a corner and we drove toward the morning sun.

Willow Falls, Midcentury

The black Ford had barely stopped at the curb when the screen door flew open and a young man appeared in the doorway. He stepped off the porch without bothering with the three shallow steps, and charged down the path to the sidewalk.

"Hey, buddy, welcome home!" he cried to the taller man emerging from the driver's side. Hurrying around the car, he wrapped both of his hands around the other's right, and pumped it vigorously. Though their height varied by several inches, there was a strong resemblance between the pair, both being broad shouldered and stocky, with sandy hair and gray-blue eyes.

"Randy! Is that really you?" A woman emerged from around the side of the house. Her obvious pregnancy hardly slowed her as she bustled up and flung her arms around the taller man's neck. "I don't believe it! We thought you had disappeared off the face of the earth! The last thing we heard from you was that you had met a girl, and then nothing! We were worried to death."

Randy Chelton smiled down at her. "Sorry, I never was much good at writing letters. But you know I always land on my feet."

He moved out of her embrace to close his car door and walk around to the passenger side. "Bill, Poppy, I'd like you to meet my wife." He reached down to open the car door and help a small dark woman to emerge. "Eloise, this is my brother Bill and his wife Poppy."

Poppy took in as many details of Eloise's appearance as she could without staring. The other woman was a few years older than Poppy, probably in her late twenties, and daintily petite. Her dark hair was brushed back from her face in a deep wave, and the crimson lipstick she wore was perfect with her coloring. Somehow she had managed to ride for hours in the car without getting wrinkles in her clothes. Eloise gave Poppy a cool smile that had the instant effect of making her feel as big as a barn and dressed in tacky rags.

Bill reached out and shook his sister-in-law's hand enthusiastically. "Eloise! It's great to meet you! Can't say I approve of your taste in men, but he's not so bad when you really get to know him. When did you all get married?"

There was a speck of silence, then Randy said, "Oh, the wedding was about a year and a half ago."

Poppy batted at him with her hand and said, "Randy! How could you get married and not let us know! Eloise, you'll have to work on his manners. But who am I to talk about manners? Here I am letting you all stand in the street. Come inside, for heaven's sake."

Eloise gave her another cool smile and started toward the house, but Randy turned and opened the car's back door. When Poppy saw what was on the back seat she gave a little shriek. "Oh! Oh my goodness, look at this! Oh, she is adorable! Let me have her. Come to your Aunt Poppy, little darlin'."

She reached into the car and lifted the baby lying in a nest of blankets into her arms. For a moment the child stiffened, but Poppy quickly nestled her into the crook of her arm and smiled at her. "Guess what, baby," she cooed, "you're going to have a cousin to play with you in a few months." The baby smiled back and reached out to grab Poppy's nose.

"Honk, honk," Bill said, laughing. "Say, Randy, this is a smart kid, he's already found Poppy's best feature."

"She, dummy," his wife said. "Don't you know a cute girl when you see one?"

"I sure do," he said, reaching out to pat his wife on her fanny.

"Eloise, what's her name?" Poppy looked around for her sister-in-law, and saw that the other woman was halfway up the path to the house. She had paused to look back at the rest of them. Poppy thought she looked like she was about to start tapping her foot impatiently.

It was Randy who answered. "Louisa," he said. "This is Louisa."

The End

If you enjoyed *Bay in the Dark*, please leave a short review or comment at this book's page on Amazon. It would be very much appreciated!

ABOUT THE AUTHOR

Sharon Henegar is the author of the Willow Falls mystery series, including *Sleeping Dogs Lie, In Dogs We Trust,* and *The Dog Prince.* Her last book was *Sidestep,* a stand-alone thriller. Her blog, *Queen of Fifty Cents,* chronicles her adventures in thrifting and was the inspiration for her book *Shopping on Driveways: Advice for Thrifters from the Queen of Fifty Cents.*

Henegar believes in home cooking, the restorative powers of humor and dogs, in buying secondhand, that a convertible should be driven with the top down, that life needs dessert, and that M&Ms should be bought in bulk.

Originally from the Midwest, Henegar now resides in a Midcentury Modern house in Salem, Oregon with her husband, Steven; Millie, a tuxedo-wearing cat; Zoe, the Springer spaniel-mix dog; and Fannie, who looks exactly like Jack.

Read on for a preview of Sharon Henegar's

Sidestep:

Chapter 1

I only meant to step out of my life for a few days. It never occurred to me that my life would be gone when I tried to step back in.

The first hint came at breakfast. I drove down to Hood River from the little cabin on the mountain where I had spent the past week. Yesterday had been blustery, cold and wet, so when dawn brought clear skies and that golden autumn sunlight that turns the world into a hazy dream, I had to put the top down on my car and take a drive.

My dog Clover was strapped into her seatbelt in the back seat. She's as tough as an old boot from all the running and retrieving she does, but at thirty pounds she would never survive a deployed airbag if I let her sit shotgun.

We stuck to backroads going down the mountain, though a short stretch on Interstate 84 was unavoidable. I rolled up all the windows to minimize the wind and kept to the right lane so I could go slower than the rest of the juggernauts speeding toward Portland. When we reached Hood River my short hair was standing on end. I batted it down, raked my fingers through it, and glanced back at Clover.

She wore the happy grin of a dog who has just had her nostrils filled with supercharged air and her ears whipped around in a frenzy. Our eyes met for a moment.

"You're welcome," I told her.

I found the breakfast café I'd Yelped on the main drag. Half a block further a car was just leaving a parking place, a nice long one that I could nose into instead of having to actually parallel park—not my best driving skill. I glanced around the interior of the car and decided I'd better put the lid back up. There were a few things I'd be sorry to have stolen, items I'd brought along on our journey from North Carolina that I didn't trust the movers to ship safely to the new place. A push of a button later the car was as secure as a ragtop gets. I grabbed Clover's leash from the seat beside me, freed her from the back seat, and led her down the street.

One small table was unoccupied on the café patio, back in a shaded corner. I sat down and dropped Clover's leash. She sniffed the area around my chair then settled at my feet, front paws crossed. Her amber eyes inspected the scene around us, and I saw her nostrils quivering as she read the secrets brought to her on the morning breeze.

"Coffee?" My waiter was of medium height and muscular, with tanned skin and ruddy cheeks. I could easily imagine him whipping his way across the Columbia with the other windsurfers. He laid a laminated menu on the table, then set down a glass of ice water.

"Hot tea," I replied. "Something black, but not Earl Grey."

"Darjeeling?"

I nodded. "And some cream, please."

He returned in about five minutes with the tea, but not the cream. "Do you know what you'd like to order?"

I handed him the menu. "A short stack of the cinnamon French toast, two eggs scrambled, and the cream for my tea."

"Oops, sorry about that." He tucked the menu under his order pad and scribbled, then looked around at the other tables. Two ladies were gathering up their purses. "Hey Janice, are you done with that cream pitcher?"

"Sure am." She rose, picked up the creamer, and held it out to him. As he took it she looked at me and said, "There's plenty left. Gina always thinks she wants cream and then never uses any."

"Thanks," I grinned back at her. I heard Clover's whippy tail thumping against my chair leg.

"That's a handsome dog. Looks like she knows a thing or two."

"Oh, she knows everything." I looked down into Clover's bright eyes. "And then some."

Janice chuckled and turned away with a little wave. My waiter set down the creamer near my teacup. "Back in a few minutes with your food."

The café got extra points when I saw I'd been given loose tea steeping in a china pot. A handsome pewter strainer sat on the cup. When I poured out the first cup, my nostrils filled with that lovely tea aroma and I gave a deep sigh. Maybe this was a good omen, and I'd been right to turn my life in an entirely new direction.

I took a sip, then reached for my purse and took out my Kindle Fire. I'd finished the book I was reading last night and needed to find a new one to try. I settled on one called *Sleeping Dogs Lie*; it sounded fun, and some of the characters were dogs. "Maybe you'll like it too, you can read it when I'm done," I told Clover. I clicked the Buy It Now button.

The next screen asked for a password.

I frowned. It never asked me for a password at this point. I had set things up with a password to get into the device, but once I was in, this particular password had been memorized.

Until today.

And I had no idea what the password was.

For a moment I regretted my decision not to use one of those online password sites. I'd opted instead to keep my own list, in a randomly named document on my laptop. I have a good memory for lots of things, but there were so many passwords to keep up with these days. Every card in your wallet had a different one, not to mention every website you interacted with, from your bank to the site where you found your knitting patterns. Like most people, I'd started out years ago using the same code for just about everything. But by now I had seen too many warnings about the necessity for unique—and frequently changed—passwords. So I had a zillion passwords and could only remember about three of them.

I just wouldn't be reading a new book through breakfast. No big deal. When I got back to the cabin I'd find my password list, buy the e-book, and be back in business.

I poured more tea and sat back, enjoying the sunshine. I inspected the other breakfasters, a varied lot. People in business suits, people in every variety of casual clothing. One large table was surrounded by a group of eight teenage girls. I caught talk about dorm rooms and class schedules. Perhaps they were high school friends getting together for the last time before heading to college.

Breakfast actually lived up to the hype I'd read about the place. My sister and I had "collected" French toast through our childhood, always ordering that when we were taken out to breakfast. We had taken our French Toast Rating System quite seriously. Feeling very Gallic, we had used up to five Eiffel Towers to denote the quality of the food. Of course, a really cute waiter could influence us to give more Eiffel Towers to a less than stellar product. I still ordered it in her memory, sending her a little mental report on how it compared.

Clover was happy as well. Our waiter brought her a heavy china bowl of water and a little plate of homemade dog biscuits. "Our dessert baker invented these for her pets," he explained, "and now every dog in town expects them when they come here."

He checked on my progress two or three times, refilling the teapot with steaming hot water without being asked. When he presented the bill he said, "No hurry, just whenever."

I fished out a credit card and laid it on top of the bill on the little tray. "Here you go." I poured out more tea into my cup, and thought about how Clover and I might spend the day.

My waiter was back at my side, proffering my credit card. "I'm sorry," he said quietly, "but this card wouldn't run. Do you have another we could use?"

"What? Are you kidding?" I shook my head and thought for a moment. "I used it a couple of days ago for gas. I wonder if they messed up the strip or something."

"Could be." He looked at me expectantly. I grabbed my purse and pulled out my billfold. "Here, this should work." I handed him the other credit card I had with me, one that I rarely use. The account had a high line of credit and I knew I hadn't charged anything on it for months.

But soon he was back again, his voice even lower. "Umm, we tried several times and the machine didn't like this one either." He handed me the card.

"Gosh," I said lightly, hoping that the uneasiness fluttering among the French toast didn't show, "I wonder what's going on. Sorry about that. Let me just give you the cash. How much was it?"

Breakfast paid for, I gathered up my purse and Clover's leash. I had planned to take a walk around Hood River, maybe go for a drive around the surrounding orchards and admire all the apples and pears waiting to be picked. But the password and credit card snafus made me decidedly uneasy. I hurried back to the car and strapped Clover into her seatbelt. The bright sunshine seemed dimmed, and the air felt like storm clouds were hiding just over the horizon...

Sidestep...available now in paperback and Kindle formats at Amazon.com!